"What will it [D0020936] **?"**

Trent tried to get [...] blackness of the [...]

She shook her head. "The only person I can rely on is myself."

But he saw the tears in her eyes and knew her walls were coming down. He glimpsed the woman lurking there, scared and alone. A fierce surge of protectiveness rose in him.

They couldn't stay here. It wasn't safe. "Let's go back to the cabin."

With hesitation, she put her hands in his. It wasn't a romantic gesture, though the idea was appealing. It was a matter of survival, the two of them sticking together in the bleak wilderness.

He led her up the mountain, but as they neared his cabin, he pulled her behind a tree, his muscles tightening as instinct kicked in. Instinct that told him something was wrong.

He nodded toward the distance. "Listen."

A crackle, followed by an explosion.

"What is that?" Tessa whispered.

"That was my cabin. It just went up in flames."

He felt Tessa shudder.

They were here. The killers had found them. Again.

Christy Barritt's books have won a Daphne du Maurier Award for Excellence in Suspense and Mystery and have been twice nominated for the RT Reviewers' Choice Best Book Award. She's married to her Prince Charming, a man who thinks she's hilarious—but only when she's not trying to be. Christy's a self-proclaimed klutz, an avid music lover and a road trip aficionado. For more information, visit her website at christybarritt.com.

Books by Christy Barritt

Love Inspired Suspense

Keeping Guard
The Last Target
Race Against Time
Ricochet
Desperate Measures
Hidden Agenda
Mountain Hideaway

The Security Experts

Key Witness
Lifeline
High-Stakes Holiday Reunion

MOUNTAIN HIDEAWAY

CHRISTY BARRITT

HARLEQUIN® LOVE INSPIRED® SUSPENSE

Recycling programs
for this product may
not exist in your area.

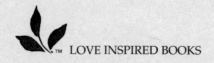 LOVE INSPIRED BOOKS

ISBN-13: 978-0-373-67726-9

Mountain Hideaway

Copyright © 2016 by Christy Barritt

www.Harlequin.com

Printed in U.S.A.

Truly I tell you, if you have faith as small as a mustard seed, you can say to this mountain, "Move from here to there," and it will move. Nothing will be impossible for you.
—*Matthew* 17:20

To all the children my husband and I work with every Sunday at Kempsville Christian—your faith inspires me. Thank you for being a part of my life.

ONE

Tessa Jones flung herself across the couch toward the lamp and pulled the switch so hard the ceramic base nearly toppled onto the wooden floor below. With quick breaths, she darted toward the wall.

She pulled her sweater closer around her neck and forced air into her lungs. Anxiety pressed down on her and adrenaline surged, the mix making her head spin.

Slowly, she edged toward the window. She had to look. She had no choice.

With all the lights extinguished in her home, anyone lurking outside shouldn't see her. Still, she had to be careful. She had no idea who or what was on the other side of that glass. Here in the middle of nowhere, there were no neighbors to hear her scream, to rush to her rescue. If something happened to her, she might not be found for days.

That had worked to her advantage...until today.

At this moment, she craved having someone nearby to help her, to be a second set of eyes. But she'd been mentally preparing for months to be self-reliant if a situation like this ever occurred. She'd only hoped it would never come to this.

As she turned toward the window, her eyes adjusted to the darkness. She stared hard yet cautiously into the abyss of thick woods surrounding the property.

Certainly, the speck of light bobbing on the horizon had just been her imagination. There was no one out there among the trees and the steep landscape of the mountain terrain. There couldn't be. No one even knew this place was here.

Blackness stared back, and her heart slowed.

It had been her imagination. Just her imagination. Maybe her paranoia. It didn't matter, as long as what she'd seen hadn't been real.

Just then something flickered in the distance.

She blinked, her momentary relief instantly vanishing. She clutched her chest as her heart thumped out of control. Despite the cold, sweat spread across her forehead.

The light was small, like a flashlight, and it continued to bob through the woods.

Someone was walking. Toward the cabin. Toward her.

Leo's men had found her, she realized.

Fear paralyzed her.

It didn't matter that she'd run through this potential scenario a million times. That she'd rehearsed what she would do. That she'd planned the best course of escape.

Right now, all of those thoughts disappeared.

She'd been here eight months. She'd thought she was safe. She'd prayed she was.

But God had stopped answering her prayers a long time ago.

The beam grew larger as it neared the property. Whoever was holding the light had probably seen the lamp on. Knew that Tessa was here. Hiding, at this point, would be fruitless.

No, she had to run.

She shook her head, thoughts colliding inside.

If she ran, the mountains would kill her, even if whoever was after her didn't. It was too dark. There were too many cliffs. Too many unknowns.

Either way, she had to move, and now!

She grabbed a backpack from her closet. She'd put it together just in case something like this ever happened. It had a flashlight, some cash, some water and a small blanket. After she slung the bag over her shoulders, she crept to the back door. She had to be decisive, to stop hesitating. If she wasn't, the person out there would reach the cabin and might hear her leave. Might sneak around to the back and catch her.

It took every ounce of her determination to pull the door open. A brisk wind blew inside. Though it was late autumn, the air felt brutally cold here in the middle of the mountains, especially at night.

She was going to miss this cabin. Miss this life.

The thought of starting over again made Tessa's head pound, made her feel as though a rock had been placed on her chest.

But she'd have time to worry about that later. Right now, she had to concentrate on surviving.

She quietly closed the door behind her. On her tiptoes, she started toward the woodshed in the distance. She'd hide out there and see what unfolded. She didn't have much choice. If the intruder came too close, she could dart into the woods. She'd take her chances there before she'd take them at the hands of the ruthless men who Leo had probably sent after her.

Ducking behind the rough wood of the shed, she crouched, desperate to stay concealed. As the wind blew, the leaves swept across the ground. The sound, normally comforting, made her nerves tighten.

She held her breath, listening for any indications of the intruder.

She heard nothing.

That was when her mind began running through scenarios and she remembered—

Her car!

Of course, anyone after her would see her car. They'd know she was here. They'd tear everything apart until they found her. And once they found her... She shuddered to think of what would happen then.

If she somehow happened to escape, they could easily trace her license plate. They'd put one and one together. She felt hunted and as if there was no safe place for her to hide. Her cubbyhole away from the world had been compromised.

She'd have to start over again with a new identity, a new home, a new everything.

How could she go on like this for the rest of her life? Living with this kind of fear wasn't living at all. It was surviving.

Just as she closed her eyes, on the verge of praying for mercy, she heard a bang. She clutched her chest. As she peered around the corner, the back door flung open.

The wind! Tessa realized.

The door had never latched easily. In her haste to get out of the house, she must not have pulled hard enough.

Now there was no hiding the fact that she was nearby. It was a matter of evading the intruder more than it was about hiding.

Despair bit deep. Maybe it would just be easier to give up.

No, Tessa reminded herself. No matter how tempting the thought might be at times, she knew she couldn't surrender. Leo didn't deserve to win, and she wouldn't go down without a fight.

Leo McAllister, her ex-fiancé, had already turned her life upside down when she'd caught him in the middle of smuggling blueprints for dangerous weapons to terrorists overseas. She'd tried to gather evidence to nail him, but she'd failed. That was when she'd known she had no choice but to run.

He'd sent men after her and they'd soon found her at the first place she'd sought refuge—an old house she'd rented with cash and a fake name. She'd discovered the cottage off a lonely country road in the rolling hills of Virginia and had thought she'd found the perfect hideaway. She'd been wrong. While coming home from buying groceries, she'd seen the men inside her temporary home and had fled.

Tessa had barely gotten away. She wouldn't have escaped if it hadn't been for a drawbridge that she'd crossed just in time.

Now Tessa waited, holding her breath, to see what would happen next. In theory, she'd been living like this ever since that life-changing day when she'd discovered Leo's true colors.

The light appeared again.

The intruder was inside her cabin now, she was certain.

A voice drifted out, but she couldn't make out the words.

As the wind brushed her again, her nose tingled. It wouldn't be too long before her ears, her cheeks and her fingers all went numb. So many things could go wrong right now.

She squinted as someone stepped out the back door. The flashlight nearly caught her, but she tucked herself back behind the shed in time. As she saw the beam fade to the other side of the property, she stole another glance.

The man on her deck was tall and broad. He wore a black coat—leather, maybe—and low-slung jeans. He didn't look familiar but, then again, it was dark. Besides, the McAllisters had enough money to hire people to do their dirty work. Leo would never do this kind of job himself.

The man stepped off the deck and walked around the side of the house. Her heart pounded in her ears as she waited for what seemed like hours. He circled the house twice. Shone his light into her car. Surveyed the area around the cabin.

Then he started toward the woods near the shed.

Tessa held her breath. *No! Not back here.*

His footsteps stopped.

Slowly, the sound faded, almost as if he was… retreating?

She counted to ten before peering around the corner again. In the distance, she saw the light disappear into the woods. He was leaving.

He was *leaving*!

But why? Maybe he wasn't one of the men after her. Maybe he was just a passerby whose car had broken down or a hunter checking out the area. Maybe he'd gotten lost on the winding road and had come looking for directions.

None of those things sounded quite true, even in her own mind, but she couldn't think too long.

Once the light disappeared well out of sight, she hurried to the house.

She'd forgotten her car keys. She had to grab them and get out of here. There was no time to waste.

She shuddered as she scrambled over the crispy leaves across her backyard. She sprinted up the steps, mentally reviewing where she'd left them. She couldn't risk turning the lights on. Relying on her memory, she rushed toward the kitchen table. Her purse was there.

Had the man seen it? Had he looked inside and seen her license?

Her hands trembled now. She snatched the bag, her gaze frantically searching the countertop for the keys. Thankfully they were right beside the coffeepot where she'd left them.

She lunged toward them and felt the metal against her fingers.

Now she just had to get out of here.

Just as she turned, she sensed someone behind her. Before she could scream, a hand covered her mouth.

And, for the first time in years, she prayed.

Trent McCabe hated to scare the woman—to scare any woman. But if he didn't grab her now, she'd run. Then he'd never have any answers to the heavy questions hanging over his head.

He couldn't let her get away. There were too many reasons why it would be a bad idea.

He kept one hand firmly over her mouth and his other arm locked her elbows against her body. He lifted her off her feet, and she kicked, flailing. But she wasn't going anywhere. Trent would give her a few minutes and, once she was worn out from struggling, he'd try to talk to her. She'd left him with very few options.

She fought against him, each jerk full of fight. He had to admire her for that. But he'd fought enough battles and had enough muscles and brawn to easily overtake her. She would wear out much sooner than he would. He just had to be patient.

She paused and her chest heaved as if she was gulping in breaths. His heart lurched as he realized just how terrified the woman was. He'd never meant for things to play out like this. He'd just been so desperate to find her.

"I'm not going to hurt you. I just have a few questions," he murmured in his most calming, apologetic voice. "Quiet down."

His words had the opposite effect and seemed to propel her back into action. She began thrashing again, trying desperately to get out of his grip. This woman wasn't going to give up, was she? She had more fight than he'd guessed.

Trent stood there, waiting patiently. But he gave her credit for her efforts. She was giving it all she had.

"Listen, your mom sent me," he finally said.

She slowed for a moment. Without even seeing her face, he knew the wheels in her brain were turning, were processing the information. That was a good sign.

"I'm going to move my hand from your mouth so we can talk. Okay?" he soothed as a tremble began shaking her muscles.

She remained where she was, her breathing too shallow for her own good.

"Okay?" he repeated.

Finally, she nodded her head.

One of his hands slipped back down to his side.

She remained eerily still, not saying a word but unable to run. He waited for her to speak.

They said good things came to those who waited, and the saying had proved to be true more than once in his life. Though it had also proved deadly. He hoped that wouldn't be the case now.

"My mom's dead," she finally said, her voice just above a whisper.

"No, she's not. You and I both know that."

"Let me go. Let's talk like two humans." Her voice shook with emotion, yet based on the tight cadence of her words, she was trying to control her fear.

Guilt flashed through him. He hated for this to be his only means of talking to her. His mom had raised him better than this. But what else was he supposed to do? Drastic situations called for drastic actions.

He had his doubts, but he realized that acting as if she was his captive wouldn't get him very far. Hesitantly, he released his clamp across her arms. "Fine. Let's talk."

As soon as she was out of his grasp, she darted to the kitchen counter and grabbed a knife from the butcher block. She held it in front of her. Even in the dark, Trent could see the desperate gleam in her gaze. "Step back."

He raised his hands. "I'm not going to hurt you."

"You break into my home, practically take

me hostage and then tell me your intentions are golden? I don't think so."

"Don't forget that I also let you go," he reminded her, willfully trying to gain her trust. He knew he could easily work that knife from her hands, but he'd scared the woman enough already. "I didn't want you to run away. That's the only reason I grabbed you like that."

"Justify it however you want. You need to get out of my house. Now." She pointed toward the door with her knife.

"I just want to talk. Besides, this isn't your house, is it?"

She held the knife higher, her chin rising in stubborn determination. "I thought I made myself clear. Get out. Now."

Trent took another step back, hoping the woman would realize he didn't want to hurt her. He couldn't blame her for doubting that. "Your mom has been searching for you."

The dark concealed her face, but he sensed her shoulders slumping. "Like I said, my mom is dead."

"You and I both know you're lying, Theresa." He watched her face as he used her name. He only wished there was more light so he could see. Any of the small hints she might offer to prove he was telling the truth were erased by the darkness.

"That's not my name." Her voice shook even harder. "I'm Tessa Jones."

"Your name is Theresa Davidson." She was thinner now. Her hair was long and light brown when it used to be shoulder length, curly and blond. But he'd been searching for six months, and he felt certain this was the woman he was looking for. "I'm Trent McCabe, by the way."

"I'm going to call the police." Her words didn't sound remotely convincing.

"Go right ahead. I'll wait here while you do it." Their conversation felt a bit like a game. He'd made his move, she'd made hers and they continued to go back and forth. Trent knew good and well that she wouldn't call the police. She had too much at stake. People who wanted to disappear did not call the police.

"Why are you doing this?" Her voice cracked with desperation. "I'm giving you the chance to leave. Please. Just go."

"You have a lot of people who are concerned about you." Seeing the worry in her loved ones' eyes had been enough to compel him to stick with this case long after the time and funds had run out. He'd seen something in her family that he'd seen in himself all those years ago: pain and hurt. If possible, he wanted to spare them any more heartache.

"You have the wrong person." She said each

word slowly, forcefully. It was almost as if she was trying to convince herself of the truth.

But Trent heard the emotion there. The doubt. The fear. The moment of hesitation. There was no question this was the right woman.

But she wasn't going to give this whole act up now. He didn't know what had driven her to come here, to hide for all these months. But it must be a strong reason.

Whatever it was, she wasn't budging. He had to think of a different approach because this one certainly wasn't working. She wasn't in the right emotional state to change her mind.

"Okay, okay. Look, I'm sorry to have scared you." He took a step backward. "I'll leave."

He kept backing up until he reached the front door. A moment of hesitation hit him, and he started to try to persuade her again, but thought better of it. The woman was spooked. The fear that he'd seen in those big blue eyes of hers would make sure that any pleas for logic would go unheard.

He couldn't actually see the blue, but he remembered it from the photos of Theresa. Her eyes had been one of her most striking features. He recalled the earnest, sincere look—it was one that couldn't be faked.

He'd guess that this woman hadn't lost that sincerity, either. The warmth in her eyes was something that was a part of her. The ability to show her character with one look, expressing deep emotions, communicating without a word.

Kind of like Laurel. His heart ached at the memory.

He gripped the doorknob, took one last look at the shadowy woman who still stood on guard and stepped outside.

Just as he did, a bullet pierced the air.

TWO

Tessa froze at the sound. Someone was shooting! There was more than one person who'd shown up here. She should have known better.

Before she could react, the man—the intruder—dived back into the house and slammed the door. "Get down!"

She must not have been moving fast enough, because he threw himself over her. The knife flew from her hand and clattered to the corner.

"We've got to get out of here!" he grumbled.

She stiffened with alarm at the very suggestion. "I'm not going anywhere with you."

"I'm not the one firing at you." His breath was hot on her cheek, and his closeness caused heat to shoot through her. She'd been so isolated that human touch seemed foreign, surreal. In order to survive, she'd been forced to keep her distance from people.

"This could all be an elaborate scheme on your

part," she said through clenched teeth. "*Elaborate* being the key word."

"I promise you that I'm on your side. I don't want to die, either, and if we stay here, that's what's going to happen." He looked at her a moment. "Can you trust me?"

"I don't even know you! Of course I can't."

"You're going to have to decide who you trust more, then—me or the men shooting outside your house."

"Neither!" Her answer came fast and left no room for uncertainty.

As a bullet shattered the front window, his gaze caught hers. "Please, Ther—Tessa. I don't want you to get hurt. Your family would be devastated if you were. These men must have followed me here."

Something in the man's voice seemed sincere, and the mention of her family softened her heart. What if they *had* hired someone to find her? She could see them going to those measures.

She'd known when she disappeared they would worry. But what else could she have done? Leo would kill them, too, if they knew too much. Leaving without giving them a reason had been the hardest thing she'd ever done.

Tessa snapped back to the present and realized that she had little choice at this point but to go along with this Trent guy. Hesitantly, she nodded. "Fine, I'll trust you for now."

"Good. Now we're getting somewhere. We've got to get out here and make it to my Jeep. I'm sure those men outside have got their eyes on the doors. Are there any other exits?"

"The basement. We can escape from the storm cellar. The door opens at the other side of the hot tub. The exit is hard to see, especially with the leaves covering the ground at this time of year."

"Perfect. Show me how to get there."

With trepidation, Tessa crawled across the floor. As she passed the iron poker by the fireplace, she briefly entertained the idea of grabbing it and knocking out the man beside her. Maybe she could get away on her own and take her chances. But Trent had proved himself to be quick and able. Besides, that would only cost them more time.

She reached the basement door and nudged it open. Blackness stared at her on the other side, so dark and thick that her throat went dry. The basement was the last place she wanted to go. But what choice did she have?

She half expected Trent to push her down the stairs, lock her in the damp space and later gloat that she'd fallen for his ruse. Ever since Leo, Tessa had a hard time trusting people. The situation at the moment felt overwhelming with all of its uncertainties.

"You'll be okay." She heard the whispered assurance from behind her.

He seemed to sense her fear. She nodded again and forced herself to continue. When she reached the first step, she stood, still hunched over and trying to make herself invisible.

Another window shattered upstairs. Someone was definitely desperate to kill her. She only hoped she hadn't trusted the wrong person.

Just as she reached the basement floor, her foot caught. She started to lunge forward when a strong hand caught her shoulder and righted her. "You okay?"

"I'm fine," she whispered, still shaky.

When her feet found solid ground, she expected to feel relief. Instead, her quivers intensified. She couldn't see anything down here. Someone could be hiding, just waiting to attack.

Trent gripped her arm. "Can you tell me where the stairway that leads outside is?"

"To the right."

He propelled her forward, not waiting for her to gather herself. Before she realized what was happening, he led her up another set of steps, through some cobwebs, and then stopped.

"Stay right here," he whispered.

With measured motions, he slid the latch to the

side and cracked the exterior door open. Moonlight slithered inside, along with a cool burst of air.

As she listened, her heart pounded in her chest with enough force that she felt certain anyone within a mile could hear it. This could be it. She could die.

Leo and his minions had finally found her. She'd known it was only a matter of time before her ex located her and ensured she remained silent about his prestigious family's dealings with terrorists.

What she wasn't sure about was this man with her now and his role in all of this. She knew this: there were people out there prowling around and searching for victims, for people to take advantage of. She'd never be that person again, not if she could help it.

The man was closer now, too close. Near enough that she could feel his body heat, that she could smell his leathery aftershave. Unfortunately, he was also close enough that she could catch a glance of his breathtaking, although shadowed, features. Even in the dark, she spotted his chiseled face, his perceptive eyes, his thick and curly hair.

"How fast can you run?" he whispered.

"I was a sprinter in high school." As soon as the words left her mouth, she clamped her lips shut. Why had she said that? Why had she given any indication of who'd she'd been in her past life, her life before hiding out here in the mountains of Gideon's Hollow, West Virginia?

"You're going to need to utilize some of those skills now," he muttered. "On the count of three, we need to make a run for it. Jump in my Jeep and go. No hesitating. No looking back. Can you do that?"

She nodded before finally choking out, "Yes, yes, I can do that."

"Take my hand." A wisp of moonlight slithered through the crack and illuminated his outstretched fingers.

She swallowed back her fears and slipped her hand into his. She'd act now and think later. She had no other choice.

"One. Two. Three!" With that, he burst out of the basement and flew like a bullet toward the woods.

She hardly had time to think, to breathe. All she could do was try to remain on her feet as trees and underbrush and boulders blurred by. Somehow she avoided falling or tripping or tumbling forward. It had something to do with the strength that emanated from the man in front of her. He seemed so in control, even in such a precarious situation.

A shout sounded in the distance. She thought

she heard more scurrying, but everything moved too fast for her to put it together. Another gunshot rang out.

Something straight ahead glinted in the moonlight. The next moment Trent pushed her inside a dark vehicle that had been concealed by the nighttime and the thick woods. Before she could catch her breath, he hopped in the driver's seat and they squealed onto the road.

Her heart pounded out of control as she tried to absorb what had just happened.

She'd just survived one attempt on her life. Now she braced herself for what this man might do with her next.

"Put your seat belt on!" Trent yelled, snapping his own in place.

Thankfully, Tessa listened, though she could barely carry out the request. Her hands trembled too badly. Finally the mechanism clicked in place.

He hit the accelerator and the tires turned against the steep, winding mountain road. This road was tricky enough in the daytime, but right now, with no overhead streetlights and dull, no longer reflective guardrails, it would be a particularly treacherous drive.

But he had to get out of here fast. Whoever was shooting at them wasn't playing around. They were shooting to kill.

Who were those men? How had they found him? And the bigger question, why did they want Tessa dead?

Trent knew he'd been careful. But something must have triggered someone with less than honorable intentions to the fact that he'd tracked down Tessa.

He'd assumed she had run away because of her broken engagement. Further digging into her past had shown she was in massive credit card debt, had lost her job and had been seeing a psychologist.

Some feared she'd lost it. There had been no signs of foul play in her disappearance. Just a note: "I have to go. Don't try to find me."

Her family didn't believe any of that, though. They feared she was in trouble. Maybe she'd seen a crime and fled. Maybe someone had forced her to write that note. Had forced the massive purchases on her credit cards.

They claimed she'd never seen a psychologist, that she was happy and one of the most stable people one could meet.

Trent had been trying to discover what was reality and what was fiction.

Had the men who were after them—whoever they were—talked to Bill Andrews after Trent?

Bill owned the cabin where Tessa was staying. Trent had questioned him about her disappearance and, as they discussed Tessa, the man had mentioned his fond memories of the times when she had come with his family to an old hunting cabin he owned in West Virginia. Bill hadn't been back in years.

On a whim, Trent had decided to check the place out. No one was supposed to be staying there. But when Trent had seen the light in the window, he'd suspected that his hunch was correct. Tessa had known about the cabin and was using it to hide out.

The vehicle outside the residence hadn't been her car. She must have gotten a new one, along with taking a new name. The woman had to be intelligent to make it as far as she had without being detected.

Maybe Bill had told those men about his cabin, just as he'd told Trent. More than likely, though, the men who were shooting at them had followed Trent here. That meant that he'd led these men right to Tessa. He should have been more careful. Maybe there was more to her story than he'd assumed.

He'd have time to think about that later. He'd promised Tessa's mom that he'd do everything in his power to bring her daughter home safely, and that was exactly what he planned on doing. He would have to formulate his moves carefully in order to make that happen.

He watched the speedometer climb, knowing these speeds weren't safe on the winding road. Beside him, Tessa was deathly quiet. He stole a glance at her and saw how pale she'd gone, saw how her knuckles were white as she gripped the seat. The woman was terrified.

His gaze flickered to the rearview mirror. Just as he feared, headlights swerved onto the road behind him. A car closed the space between them by the second.

"Hold on!" Trent gripped the steering wheel as he pressed the accelerator even harder.

"Are you trying to get us killed?" Tessa's voice sounded thin and fraught with tension.

"The exact opposite, actually." He saw the car behind them gaining speed, nearly close enough to rear-end them. One bump could send his Jeep into the massive rock wall beside them. One nudge could propel them to their death. He'd seen fatal car accidents plenty of times before, from back when he'd worked patrol.

He couldn't let that happen now. There weren't many options for what he could do out here, but thankfully his training in the military and as a detective had taught him a thing or two. The road didn't have many intersections and the nearest one was probably three miles away, at least. That meant he had three miles of trying to drive faster and with more control than the guys behind him. It was the only way he'd outwit them.

He continued to gun it, careful to stay in control. Tessa let out a soft moan beside him. "I can't watch."

"Probably a good idea."

"Do you have a gun?"

He resisted the urge to glance her way and try to read her expression. He couldn't afford to take his eyes off the road. But what in the world was she getting at? "I do."

"Where is it?"

"In my jacket."

Before he realized what was happening, Tessa reached into his coat and pulled out his Glock.

"What are you doing?" Alarm captured his voice.

"Trying to stay alive," she muttered. She rolled down the window, and gusts of frigid air whipped inside the Jeep. With more guts than he'd realized the woman had, she leaned outside and fired the first shot.

The car behind him swerved.

"Where did you learn to shoot like that?" he shouted over the wind.

"I've been taking lessons."

The car behind them quickly righted and charged even closer. Tessa fired again, and the sound of rubber skidding across the road filled the air. The car kept coming. Just then, the back glass of the Jeep shattered.

The men were shooting back. If they managed to pierce a tire, Trent and Tessa would be goners.

A bend in the road appeared. The area was even narrower with a cliff on one side and a rock wall on the other. This was their only chance.

Trent braced himself. "Hold on!"

He grabbed Tessa and pulled her inside before she got herself killed.

Ahead, the trees disappeared and the night-time sky was all that was visible. Tessa sucked in a deep breath beside him.

This was a twenty-five-miles-per-hour curve. He remembered it well. It was sharp, merciless and adorned with several danger-ahead signs.

He had to think quickly.

Instead of slowing down, he gunned it. They charged toward the open sky ahead. One wrong move and they'd free-fall off the mountain. It was a chance he had to take, especially since the other option meant certain death.

God, be with us!

"You're going to kill us!" Tessa screamed.

At the last minute, he jerked the wheel to the right. The Jeep skidded, nearly going into a spin.

His heart pounded out of control as the edge of the cliff neared. The car fishtailed, started to right itself, but suddenly spun.

Trent held his breath, lifting up more prayers. *Lord, please help us stop in time. Our lives depend on it.*

THREE

Tessa opened her mouth but the scream stuck in her throat. As the Jeep veered closer and closer to the edge of the mountain, her life flashed before her eyes. Her regrets. Her time apart from her loved ones. Everything she'd been through over the past year.

She didn't want things to end this way.

God, please! It was the second time today she'd found herself praying, something she hadn't done in months. Maybe it was time to change that.

Suddenly, the Jeep righted itself. Before three seconds had even passed, she felt Trent press the gas again. They accelerated down the road, her heart pounding radically out of control with each second of forward motion.

She looked over her shoulder just in time to see the car behind them swerve. The tires screeched before the horrible sound of metal hitting metal filled the air.

Her eyes squeezed shut as the vehicle charged over the edge of the cliff.

Tessa felt the color drain from her face as a sick feeling gurgled in her stomach.

"You okay?" Trent stole a glance her way.

She nodded, still shaky and queasy. "I guess."

"At least they're not following us anymore."

"That's one positive." She couldn't think of many. She'd been plucked from her obscure life and into a nightmare. Now she was hanging on for dear life on a thrill ride she'd never wanted to be a part of.

Someone was clearly trying to send a message.

She'd been discovered, and now she was in a Jeep with a stranger who might or might not be trying to kill her. For all she knew, this man was a part of this elaborate scheme. Maybe his plan involved earning her trust just so he could stab her in the back. Some people got their kicks that way.

Just then Trent pulled off the main road and onto a smaller one. They snaked through the mountains, turning a couple more times before they reached a driveway similar to the steep, narrow one that had led to her own cabin.

She didn't ask questions, though her mind raced as she tried to process everything. She needed a plan, just in case things turned ugly. She'd have to take her chances and run if this man turned out to be a thug. The woods were more survivable during the day when she could see what was coming. She'd even risk plunging herself into the wilderness at nighttime if she had to. It wasn't ideal. But she'd do that before she surrendered.

The man stopped in front of three cabins, cut the engine and turned to stare at her.

When he didn't say anything, she cleared her throat. "Where are we?"

He nodded toward the closest cabin. "This is where I'm staying while I'm in town. I rented all three."

"All three? Why did you do that?" Was it because he'd brought others with him? Because he wasn't a one-man operation, as he'd claimed? She felt as if the wool had been pulled over her eyes again.

"I just saved your life. Maybe you can stop thinking the worst of me," Trent said.

Her throat tightened at his easy assessment of her. "Why would you say that?"

"Your feelings are written all over your face. And to answer your questions, I rented all three cabins to lessen the chance that anyone would find me or ask questions. I paid in cash. The only person who should know I'm here lives in Texas. He keeps these for friends to use during hunting season."

Despite his explanation, Tessa rubbed her

arms, realizing just how isolated she was out here. Trent could kill her, dispose of her body and no one would find her for weeks. "I see."

"Let's go inside and talk." Trent's voice left no room for argument.

He started to get out, but Tessa froze where she was, fight or flight kicking in. Once she left the safe confines of the car, there was no going back. Was this really a good idea?

"Tessa?" He paused and stared at her, peering into the open door.

"What about those men who followed us?" She replayed the bullets, the chase, the car going over the cliff.

"They're dead. We have some time."

"Who are they?" she whispered, realizing the timing in all of this. It couldn't be coincidental that Trent had showed up on the very day she'd been discovered by Leo's men.

"I was hoping you could tell me."

"All of this trouble didn't start until you arrived."

"Please, come inside so we can talk." His voice softened, almost as if she was exhausting him.

She shook her head, still needing more reassurance. "I could be walking into a trap."

"I'd love to tell you more. But we're safer inside."

Finally, she nodded. She was only biding her

time right now. Trent could easily overpower her if he wanted to. He was simply being polite at the moment.

Nausea rose in her gut as he led her to a cabin. Was she out of her mind doing this? What other choice did she have? If she hadn't willingly come, no doubt Trent would have found a way to drag her here against her will.

Still, a small part of her wanted to hear what he had to say.

After all, he'd mentioned her mom. He'd had opportunity to kill her already and he hadn't done it.

Lord, if You're there and if You're listening, please be with me. Give me wisdom.

Even though she knew her words probably fell on deaf ears, hope pricked her heart. Right now she wanted to believe again, and that was more than she'd felt in a long time. Funny the things desperation could do to a person. She'd been desperate for a long time, but the word had taken on a new meaning today.

Tessa stepped inside the old cabin. It was small, with only a tiny kitchen, a cozy living room and an upstairs loft, which was probably the bedroom. The walls were made of wood planks, and everything had a rustic feel to it, from the hunter green accessories to the brown leather couch.

"I'm not going to waste time with formalities or

by offering you something to drink," Trent started. "Have a seat and let's get down to business."

Tessa nodded as he led her to the couch. He sat a respectable distance away, his gaze intense as he observed her. He reminded her a bit of a soldier, only without the uniform. He looked tough and strong and like someone she didn't want to mess with.

"Tessa, your family hired me to find you. They're very concerned about you."

She wanted to deny she had a family, but instead she listened.

"I've been searching for you for six months and my investigation finally led here. Aside from being a PI, I'm a former detective from Richmond, Virginia. Before that, I was an army ranger. I've had more than my fair share of experience when it comes to tracking down people, whether they're terrorists or runaways."

She wanted to ask a million questions. How had he found her? She'd been so careful. There was no trail.

But obviously someone else besides Trent had discovered her, as well. Was there anywhere she'd be safe? Ever?

"I have no idea what's going on, but I'm hoping you can fill in some of the blanks," Trent finished.

She opened her mouth, almost desperate to

pour out the truth to someone. It had been so long since she'd had a listening ear, and it was so hard not having anyone to speak with about the things that burdened her heart.

Feeling Trent's watchful gaze and realizing he was waiting for her response, she shook her head. "I don't know what you're talking about. I wish I could help. I do. But you have the wrong person."

His gaze remained fixated on her. Agitation stirred there. "Why are you playing these games?"

He wasn't going to easily take no for an answer, was he? If she'd thought Trent was just a pushover who'd accept her explanation and leave her alone, she was wrong. Despite that realization, she repeated, "As I said, you have the wrong person."

"Tessa, you and I both know that's not true."

Her chin trembled as she tried to subdue her emotions. She'd always been a terrible liar, even after rehearsing this speech for nearly a year. "This is a horrible misunderstanding. I'm sorry you've gone through so much trouble. As soon as I can get my car, I'll be out of your hair—"

He leaned closer. "If this is a misunderstanding, why were those men trying to kill you?"

She swallowed deeply, trying to compose herself. Otherwise, her words would come out jumbled and high-pitched and give away the fact that she knew more than she admitted. "Says the man who broke into my home. Now I'm alone in a cabin with him and no one else knows I'm here. That's enough to scare any woman. Let's face it—you're just as much of a threat as those men were."

He didn't move, didn't flinch. He just continued to stare, intense and focused. "You're right. I'm not the only person you should be scared of," he reminded her, his eyes cloudy, almost angry, yet very controlled at the same time. "You're saying you have no idea who those men were?"

Tessa shook her head, trying to protect herself and buy time until she could figure out another plan. "None. Maybe they had the wrong person, just like you."

It was true. She'd never seen those men before. But her gut told her they were Leo's friends. They'd finally found her, despite her best efforts.

When she'd gone on the run, she'd remembered her best friend's family had a cabin out here that they never used anymore. She'd even remembered where they left the key. Using the place had been a no-brainer. Tessa had simply had the power turned back on and asked to have the bills sent to the West Virginia address.

She'd found a job at a travel agency in the small town, and was able to earn just enough to pay her electrical bill, buy groceries and tend to a few other necessities. Her plan had seemed perfect.

Trent stood and began pacing in front of her. "We're not going to get very far if you don't tell me the truth, Tessa."

She rubbed her hands, now sweaty, against her jeans. "I'm sorry you've gone through all of this trouble. I don't know what else to say. I didn't ask you to get involved. You're going to have to tell your client that you were unsuccessful, even after six months."

Her poor mom. To pay for all of Trent's work, she'd probably had to drain her savings account. It would be just one more hardship her family had to endure. How much could they take? Tessa certainly didn't wish any of this on them.

But she had to think of the bigger picture. She'd rather her mom be poor and worried than dead and buried.

Finally, Trent stopped pacing. His hands went to his hips as he assessed her again. "Fine. You're free to go, then."

Tessa stood, trying to gather her courage.

There was a part of her that wanted to trust Trent, that wanted someone to help her out of this situation. Yet she knew it was better to face hardship by herself, to make her own way.

"Great." Her voice trembled as she rose. She stepped toward the door, a million possibilities racing through her head. All of them seemed to end in disaster.

"You know it's ten miles until you reach town."

She nodded, her throat dry. "I know."

"It's dark."

She nodded again, her anxiety growing into a bigger hollowness by the moment. "I realize that."

She took another step when he grabbed her arm.

"You're one stubborn woman. You're still going to set out on your own? Even after everything that's happened?"

She only stared at him.

Finally, he dropped his hand. "Look, we didn't get started on the right foot. I don't think you should go. It's not safe. Stay in one of the cabins here, okay? No strings attached. I just don't want to see anything happen to you. Understand?"

She stared at him, trying to measure his sincerity. Her emotions clouded her judgment at the moment, though, and she didn't know what to say. She really had no other options, and certainly he knew that.

"Whether you claim to be Theresa or not, your family won't survive me coming back to them with the news that you're dead. So do this for their sakes, not mine."

His words got to her. Images of her family flashed through her mind, and finally she nodded. "Okay, but not because of this family you keep on talking about. I'll do it because I hate the dark."

Her gut twisted as she said the words. Her family was the most important thing in her life. Everything she'd done, she'd done for them.

She hoped they'd forgive her for all the hurt she'd caused.

Trent stared at the woman in front of him, wishing she would come to her senses. Why was she being so stubborn? Even while dealing with her fear, he'd noticed how she continually lifted her chin, as if she was just humoring him.

There was no denying that the woman had gumption—or that she was easy on the eyes, even with her new look. He actually liked her hair the darker shade. He'd always appreciated the more natural look. The other pictures he'd seen, she'd been dressed in business suits, with expensive-looking haircuts and perfectly coordinated accessories.

The woman before him now was absent of makeup. She wore jeans, layers of a T-shirt, a henley and a flannel shirt. Her boots were small enough to look feminine, but also well worn. The change in her was remarkable. She'd more than changed her physical appearance. Her desperation and need for survival had changed her from someone who was pampered into someone practical.

Despite how frustrating she was, Trent couldn't stand the thought of her striking out on her own again. He was certain the woman was in danger, and he didn't know why yet. Her fiancé—former fiancé—had told Tessa's family that she'd had a mental break. According to Leo McAllister, one minute they'd been talking about the wedding and the next she'd gone crazy. She'd begun throwing things, accusing him of things. Leo had tried to stop her, but she'd taken off. No one had seen her since then.

Trent had known going into this that he might be confronting someone who'd flown off their rocker. But when he looked at Tessa, that wasn't the impression he had.

Was he so drawn to this case because of Laurel? It was the only thing that made sense. Guilt had been eating at him for years. He'd thought he had the emotion under control. But something about Tessa's big blue eyes made him travel back in time. Flashes of that horrible day continued to assault him and try to take him away.

He couldn't afford to immerse himself in the guilt and grief right now.

And he didn't want anyone else to go through it.

"I'll show you to your cabin, then." He put his

hand on Tessa's back and led her to the door. He figured she would object, that she'd flinch until his hand slipped away. But she didn't.

Her eyes had gone from fearful to dull. He'd seen that look before, the one that came when emotions were overwhelming, when they'd hammered a person so much that they began to feel like a shell of who they'd once been. He'd been there before.

He unlocked the cabin door and pushed it open. Even though he'd been keeping an eye on the place and felt certain no one knew he was here, he still instructed Tessa to stay where she was. Then he checked out every potential hiding place before deeming the cabin clear.

"Will this be suitable?" he asked her.

She nodded, her arms crossed protectively over her chest. "Yes."

"Tessa, I'm sorry."

"For what?" she questioned.

He shook his head, trying to find the right words. "For whatever you went through."

She opened her mouth as if to object but then closed her lips again.

He took a step toward the door when he heard her speak again.

"What do I do now? Just wait here? Indefinitely? Until those men find me again?"

He turned, praying he'd know what to say.

"That's up to you, Tessa. You can let me help or you can keep denying who you are. Things will move a lot faster if you just tell me the truth."

She stared at him. A moment of complacency flashed in her eyes. Then stubborn determination reappeared. "If I had something to tell you, I would."

He stepped closer, wishing she would stop playing these games. "You know more than you're letting on."

They stared at each other in a silent battle of wills.

Finally Trent nodded. She would tell him in her own time, and that was that. Until then, he'd do his best to keep her safe.

"Have it your way, then," Trent said.

Her face softened with…surprise? "I'm going to bed."

He stepped toward the hallway, feeling crankier than he should. He'd sacrificed a lot to come here—time, his own money, in some ways his reputation. He hoped it wasn't all for naught. "Maybe some sleep will give you a fresh perspective."

Even better, maybe some sleep would give him perspective, because a lot of the conclusions he'd drawn before coming here were proving to be dangerously incorrect.

* * *

An hour later, Tessa still stared at the space around her, feeling a mix of both uneasiness and relief—uneasiness at being here and the circumstances that had led to it and relief that she was away from Trent.

Had her mom really hired him to find her? Tessa had known her family wouldn't give up easily. But she'd hoped to hide away so well that there was no hope of that ever happening.

She paced the room, knowing she wouldn't get any sleep tonight. Not after everything that had happened. It wasn't even a slight possibility.

In the light of the cabin she'd gotten a better look at Trent. He was tall, broad and appeared to be made of solid muscle. His hair was blond with a tint of red, curly and cropped close. When his lip had started to twist up, she'd thought she'd seen a dimple on the left cheek of his very defined face.

Sure, he was handsome. Very handsome.

But sometimes a wolf looked like a sheep…or, in this case, like a ruggedly handsome Ken doll. That made him even more dangerous.

Pushing aside those thoughts, she realized that she needed to learn the lay of the house. That way, if she needed to run or hide, she at least had an idea of what her possibilities were.

The living room was simple and outfitted like most rental properties would be. There was a well-used leather couch, several magazines on the outdated coffee table and a small dinette nestled against the wall in the kitchen.

She headed toward the bedroom, determined to check that all of the windows were locked. She had to remain on guard and careful. But as soon as she stepped into the room, she stopped.

The painting on the wall.

It was by Alejandro Gaurs.

His paintings were exclusive to the world-renowned McAllister Gallery.

The art gallery that Leo's family owned.

Her breath caught.

Had she been tricked? Did Leo own this cabin? Whoever did had obviously bought the artwork at his gallery.

What if Trent had tricked her? What if he really was working for Leo?

That had to be it, she realized. Trent had convinced her that her mom had sent him, but that was all a lie. He was working for the enemy. He'd led her right into the lion's den.

Panic rose in her.

She couldn't take this risk.

She had to get out of here. Now.

FOUR

Tessa grabbed her backpack and slipped out the back door, trying to remain in the shadows. She looked toward Trent's cabin then toward the woods, but saw no one.

Moving quietly, she headed for the trees. As soon as she took her first step into the depths of the forest, she realized what a precarious place she was in. These woods could kill her.

But it was a chance she had to take.

Everything inside her told her to run fast, but she knew she had to take it slow. She couldn't be careless. One wrong step and she could break a bone. Even worse, she could fall to her death from one of the many cliffs in the area.

Slow and steady won the race. That was the saying, at least.

As Tessa left every bit—however small—of security behind, her trembles deepened. How was she going to get out of this situation? How would she last out in the wilderness? She'd read books on surviving out in nature, but everything she'd learned seemed to leave her thoughts. She only hoped the information would return as instinct kicked in.

That same intuition had kicked in when she'd grabbed Trent's gun in the car. All of those days at the shooting range had paid off. She'd been unable to buy her own gun—she'd never get past the background check, especially not with her fake name. But at least she'd picked up a few valuable skills in the process.

Tessa manipulated herself between the massive oak trees, over boulders and down steep declines. This area was so vast, so wild, so beautiful. But it could also be deadly, especially in the pitch-black. A hunter had died only a few months ago when he'd gotten lost out here. His body had been found downstream a week later.

Her mind churned as she continued her trek. When she started to maintain a steady pace, her thoughts went from survival to Trent McCabe and that painting she'd found in the cabin. It linked him to the McAllisters.

Leo was a powerful man. He was capable of extraordinary farces that could fool the wisest of people. He had to have some connection with that cabin. It was too much of a coincidence otherwise.

How had she been fooled again? The kindness

in Trent's voice was deceitful. He'd sounded so trustworthy. He'd even used a story about her mother. He probably knew how to manipulate. Those were the worst kind of criminals, the ones who gained a person's trust only to stab them in the back. Sometimes literally.

She squeezed her eyes shut at the memories.

Just then, something snapped behind her.

She froze. What was that? A nighttime creature? A mountain lion? A bear?

Her pulse spiked again.

She looked for the reflection of eyes—either human or animal predator—but saw no one. Was something stalking her out there, just waiting for the right moment to pounce?

Tessa picked up her pace. Slow and steady only worked if a person wasn't being chased.

She had a phone in her backpack. But who would she call? Who could she trust to help her?

No one, she realized. Except her family, and she couldn't pull them into this.

As she glanced around, every direction looked the same. Which route led away from her cabin? Which path would keep her safe from the deadly bluffs that dropped hundreds of feet to the river below? One moment of distraction and now she was turned around. She'd lost her sense of direction.

Panic began to rise in her.

Another twig snapped in the distance.

She was definitely being followed.

By Leo's men? By Trent—who was also one of Leo's men, apparently? By an animal?

None of the options were comforting.

Despite her earlier mantra of remaining slow, she burst into a run. She had to move, and fast. Every second she lingered could cost her life.

Branches slapped her in the face, gnarled tree roots reached out to trip her and rocks tried to twist her ankle. She pushed forward, her breathing too shallow for her own good.

She could feel a presence behind her now, sense that her pursuer was closing in.

Just then, her foot caught on another root. She started to lunge forward but caught herself on the rough bark of a pine tree.

She gasped as the prickly wood cut into her skin, as her ankle throbbed.

Tears tried to push from her eyes—from even deeper than that. They tried to push up from the deepest part of her heart, which felt too battered and bruised for words. She was so tired of living in fear, of constantly looking over her shoulder.

"Tessa!" someone said.

She knew that voice.

Trent.

Of course he'd been watching her. He'd probably just been waiting for her to run. But why was he drawing this out? Why didn't he just kill her while he had the chance?

Unless there were other motivations at play.

Did he plan to torture her? Find out how much she knew? Whom she might have told? Where she might have hidden any documents she'd kept as proof of what Leo's family had been doing?

The thought caused a new surge of panic in her.

She pushed herself from the tree and hobbled forward. Kept moving. What other choice did she have?

She tried to keep her eyes on the ground, to watch her steps. But it was so dark out here. There were so many trees and so much underbrush.

"I won't let you out of my sight, you know," the man called.

She looked behind her again and spotted Trent. He walked toward her, his actions measured and controlled. He wasn't even panting with exertion as he took long strides her way. Meanwhile, her legs kept pumping as she tried to keep pace.

Fabulous.

"Just leave me alone!" she mumbled.

"I don't want to hurt you, Tessa."

"You can't prove that." She stopped trying to run. Even though she'd been jogging every day and trying to build up both her strength and endurance, the upward climb on the mountain was doing a number on her legs and lungs. Her ankles throbbed. Her lungs refused to get enough oxygen to fill them.

She'd done a lot of things in preparation for a moment just like this—shooting lessons, working out, reading survival guides and forming emergency procedures. All of her planning seemed to disappear into a haze, though.

Fear and exhaustion did terrible things to people; the emotion robbed them of any security. It didn't seem as if that long ago she'd been confident and self-reliant and living her dream life. Today she was always looking over her shoulder, questioning every move and second-guessing every decision.

How had an ordinary girl living an ordinary life somehow turned into this? This wasn't supposed to happen. She should still be at home with her family. Still working in the art museum. Back then, life had seemed so safe and comfortable. What she wouldn't give to go back and return to the way it used to be.

That wasn't an option, though. She had to keep fighting. She couldn't let her enemies win.

Speaking of enemies, Trent was getting closer—close enough to grab her.

Suddenly, some kind of survival instinct took over. Adrenaline surged in her, giving her a strength she didn't know she had. She sprinted through the darkness.

Don't let him catch you.

"Being out here isn't safe, Tessa," Trent continued. "Let's talk this out."

She rounded a bend of trees and, before she knew what was happening, the ground crumbled beneath her.

She desperately grabbed the air, trying to find anything possible to grip on to as she slid downward. Failure meant she'd slip to her death, hundreds of feet to the river below.

It was too late: her life flashed before her eyes.

"Tessa!" Trent saw Tessa disappear, and panic engulfed him. He charged toward her, no longer fearful of jolting her into doing something stupid. She'd already done that.

He rushed toward the decline and peered down, expecting the worst. His heart slowed, but only temporarily. There she was, hanging on to a tree root, her eyes wide with despair.

"I'm going to get you up, Tessa. Just hold tight." He dropped to his stomach, trying to secure himself so he could grab her.

She moaned, her eyes squeezing shut. "Why don't you just kill me now? Why are you drawing this out and pretending to be a good guy?"

He grabbed her wrist. "I *am* a good guy."

"You've fooled me once. Not again." She refused to let go of the root she held on to.

What was she talking about? This wasn't really the time to argue. This was the time to get her to safety. "Let me help you. Then you can ask me whatever it is you want."

"You work for Leo McAllister."

His muscles tightened from the strain of trying to grab her, of trying to make sure her grip didn't slip and send her plunging to her death. "Leo has been worried about you. He put up a monetary reward for your return. But I'm not working for him."

"What?" Her voice sounded breathless.

Her wrist slipped. He needed a better grip and a little cooperation from her or they'd both end up tumbling down the mountainside. "I'd be happy to chat more in a minute. Right now, I need to make sure you don't die."

"Stop playing games—"

Before she could argue anymore, he grabbed her arm with both of his hands and heaved her onto the ledge. She landed beside him, and they both sprawled backward onto the hard rock beneath them. Silence fell between them as they each sucked in air.

That had been close. Too close.

Trent willed his heart to slow, but his adrenaline was still pumping at the close call. With one more deep breath, he propped himself up on one elbow and turned toward Tessa. "Why would you think I'm working for Leo?"

She cringed as if in pain but still managed to scowl. She pushed herself up also, rubbing her wrist as if it was sore. "One of the paintings from his gallery is hanging in that cabin."

"If I understand correctly, the paintings from his galleries are sold all over the world. *Prints* of them are sold all over the world. I do know that much."

"It's too big of a coincidence."

"There is such thing in life as a coincidence, darling. That's what this is. I'm not working for Leo or his family. I take it that would be a bad thing if I were?"

She stared into the distance, resting her arms on her knees. "I've already said too much."

"What's it going to take for you to trust me?" He peered at her, trying to get a better look at her face in the deep blackness of the forest.

"The only person I can rely on is myself."

"Your mom is Florence. She loves lilacs, makes the world's best chicken Parmesan and she has your eyes. Your sister looks more like your dad, who died of cancer five years ago. He was a good man. Quiet, a hard worker and he could build anything out of wood."

Tears glistened in her eyes. Finally, some of her walls were coming down. He was able to see beyond her facade, and the woman lurking there was broken, scared and alone.

A fierce surge of protectiveness rose in him.

He had to keep pushing. The mention of Leo had caused a reaction in her; it was his best lead. "Your family trusts Leo."

Suddenly, she straightened. "What do you mean?"

"I mean that Leo has been working with your mom to find you. He seems very concerned."

She let out a moan and ran a hand over her face. "But Leo didn't hire you? That's what you're saying?"

He shook his head. "No. Your family hired me."

"Does Leo know where you are?" Fear crackled in her voice.

"No one knows where I am. I update your mom weekly. Last she heard, I was in the DC area. Coming here was a last-minute hunch. I wanted to be certain before I gave her any hope." If Leo really was the bad guy here, just as Tessa seemed to be claiming, had he used his supposed concern for Tessa as a ruse for following Trent here and locating her himself? It was a possibility he had to consider.

Tessa's head dropped into her hands, and for the first time since he'd met her, she looked defeated, ready to give up. At least, ready to cry.

He needed to do something to relinquish her defeat. Sitting here wouldn't help, and he didn't know her well enough to give her a hug.

Finally, he stood. They couldn't sit here all night. It wasn't safe. "Let's go back to the cabin. Please. We can talk there, make sure you're okay and figure out what happens next."

With hesitation, she put her hands into his. It wasn't a romantic gesture, though she was certainly beautiful enough that the idea could be entertaining. No, it was a matter of survival, of the two of them sticking together in the middle of this bleak wilderness.

He glanced her over, looking for a sign of broken bones, of deep cuts. "Are you hurt?"

She shook her head, her expression still listless. "Only my ego."

"Stay close to me. Understand? Next time you might not be so lucky."

She nodded. Without saying anything else, he led her up the mountain, taking it slow this time. His thoughts turned over what she'd said. Whether she'd meant to or not, she'd given him insight into her past. She'd all but admitted that she really was Theresa Davidson. She did know Leo. Yet, all of that noted, she seemed terrified.

He needed to get to the bottom of her story, but now wasn't the time to do so. He needed to take her somewhere safe. He hated to see a woman look this frightened, to see someone this shaken. If there'd been a different way to do things, he would have changed his plan of action. If he'd known earlier what he knew now, his approach would have been different. But what was done was done.

As they neared his cabin, he pulled Tessa behind a tree, his muscles tightening as instinct kicked in. That instinct told him that something indiscernible was wrong.

"What it is?" Her eyes were as wide as the full moon overhead.

He put a finger over his lips and nodded toward the distance. "Listen."

Silence stretched—the only sounds were that of dry leaves clicking together and rustling in the breeze. Occasionally, an owl hooted or a squirrel scampered past.

Then he heard it again. A crackle. He exchanged a glance with Tessa. She'd heard it, also.

A roar sounded. A burst. An explosion.

"What is that?" Tessa whispered.

"That was my cabin. It just went up in flames."

FIVE

A shudder rippled through Tessa.

They were here. Those men had found them. Again.

She looked over her shoulder. Their pursuers could be anywhere. They could be within reaching distance. Their guns could be pointed at Tessa and Trent now.

Trent's hand on her shoulder brought her back to reality.

"What are we going to do?" Her voice sounded as raw as her throat felt.

She'd said *we*, she realized. Somewhere in the process she'd decided she was in it with Trent. She had little choice in the matter, it seemed. Not if she wanted to stay alive.

"We need to lie low until we know the coast is clear." He took her arm. "Come on. Let's start moving."

She wanted to argue, wanted to give a million reasons why venturing back into the woods was a bad idea. But she didn't. Almost on autopilot, or perhaps it was the shock—whatever it was kept her moving silently through the woods. She was too scared to stop, too charged with adrenaline to grow weary, too on edge to feel safe. Even the autumn chill didn't bother her as much as it normally would.

They moved briskly through the woods, putting distance between themselves and the flames. Where would they go? They couldn't go back to Trent's Jeep. Besides, the tires were probably melted from the heat of the blazing inferno that used to be Trent's cabin.

But Trent and Tessa couldn't meander through these woods all night, either. Trent might be built like a soldier—a very handsome soldier—but he was still human. She couldn't expect him to work wonders.

"Salem," she muttered. The older gentleman's kind eyes fluttered through her memory, solidifying her idea.

Trent looked back at her. "What?"

"We're going to need help. I bet Salem would let us borrow one of his cars."

"Who's Salem?"

"He owns the hardware store in town. He only lives a mile away from my cabin."

"You sure you can trust him?"

She nodded, not a single doubt in her mind.

"Yes, I'm sure. Believe me, people go through a rigorous criteria with me before I'm able to put any faith in them. Experience has taught me it's better that way."

Trent nodded. "Okay. We need to figure out how to get to his place."

"It was west of my cabin, just a little farther down the road."

Of course, a mile in this terrain was different than a mile of highway. Especially at night. So many things could go wrong.

He froze and put a finger over his lips. Prickles danced across Tessa's skin and she held her breath. What did he hear?

She scooted closer to him. That was when she heard it, too. A twig snapped in the distance.

Trent grabbed her hand and tugged her closer. Quietly, they moved toward a grove of trees. Trent pulled her between a huge boulder and a fortress of foliage, then squeezed in beside her. They both remained motionless.

Tessa could hardly breathe as she waited to see what would unfold. Maybe it was just a wild animal they'd heard and not one of the men desperate to kill them.

Just as the thought entered her mind, she heard another movement. The sound was so subtle that she thought she'd imagined it. But then she heard the rustling again. And again.

Someone was walking. Close. The footsteps seemed to barely hit the ground, but the crunch of dry leaves gave them away.

Tessa felt Trent squeeze in beside her. He was near enough that she could feel his heart beating at a steady rhythm against her arm. She could feel the heat coming from him.

"We lost them," a deep voice muttered in the distance.

Silence passed and Tessa could sense the man following them was within arm's reach.

"I don't know how they got away, but I've been searching this mountain for an hour," the man continued. "They must have had a car hiding somewhere, because they're gone."

Another moment passed. The man was talking on the phone to someone, Tessa realized. Leo, maybe?

"Somehow they got out of the cabins before the bomb went off. This guy who's helping her is good. He's making our job harder."

Tessa's heart stuttered, suddenly grateful that this stranger beside her had shown up when he had. She'd be dead without him.

"I know, I know. This woman has taken up too much of our time and energy. We need to put this behind us, and there's only one way to do that," the man said. "Don't worry, I'm not giving up. You can count on me."

At that, the footsteps retreated.

But neither Tessa nor Trent budged. Because one wrong move and they could both die.

Trent waited at least fifteen minutes. He figured that was a safe passage of time to ensure the man chasing them was gone and this wasn't some elaborate trap. This whole situation ran a lot deeper than he'd realized. The danger that had been chasing them was far greater than he'd guessed.

At least Tessa seemed to trust him—however reluctantly—a little more. She hadn't scowled at him in the past hour. She hadn't argued when he instructed her to hide in the woods. That was a start, he supposed.

It had brought him unexpected delight when her gaze had softened, and he'd seen something shift inside her. But it scared him that his joy went deeper than the satisfaction over gaining her trust. Something about the woman intrigued him.

When the coast seemed to be clear, he crawled out of the hiding spot. Thank goodness the little nook had been there. Finding it had been a blessing of God. Without it, they would have certainly been discovered.

Trent surveyed the area once more before motioning for Tessa to follow. "We're not going to last very long out here in these woods. I hate to say it, but I think we need to go to your friend's house tonight. By tomorrow morning it might be too late."

"Too late? What do you mean, too late?"

"I'm saying that if you were close to this Salem man, then anyone after us is likely to discover that information. They'll tear apart every area of your life here. They may go after him next, trying to get some information from him about you."

She gasped. "No, not Salem. I can't let anyone else get hurt because of me. I just can't."

"Let's go there now and warn him."

She nodded, looking numb still. Anyone whose life had been turned upside down like this would feel the same way. Before she could think too much, Trent led her back in the direction of her cabin. Traversing these mountains and woods would make the journey take longer, but they couldn't risk walking alongside the road.

Tessa was a trouper. Though the night was cold, she kept moving, kept pushing ahead. Sometimes the walk was treacherous, but she didn't let that deter her. The woman was stronger than he'd given her credit for, and he could admire that.

"We're getting closer to your cabin," he said. "You said Salem lives a mile away, correct?"

She nodded. "I'm turned around, though. I feel as if every direction I look is the same."

"I can get you there." He glanced at the compass on his watch. "The road is about a half a mile south of us and we've been walking parallel to it. If we keep going in this direction, we should hit his property soon."

"I'm glad you know what you're doing. How do you know what you're doing?"

"I was a ranger. Survival is one of the top priorities."

"You saved my life tonight."

"Actually, if you hadn't run from that cabin when you did, we could both be dead. They were going to kill you and then me to ensure I didn't talk."

"They're ruthless like that."

"Who are 'they,' exactly?"

He saw the veil go up around her again. He had a feeling that would happen every time he brought up the past.

"Leo hired them to kill me."

Her answer made him blanch. She actually had opened up and, boy, had it been a doozy. "Say that again?"

"My ex-fiancé, Leo McAllister, hired men to kill me. That's why I've been on the run."

Of all the things he'd thought she might say, that wasn't one of them. "Why in the world would he do that?"

"I walked in on his family as they were planning to do an arms deal."

"What?" Certainly he hadn't heard her correctly.

She nodded. "The family doesn't care about art. Beneath their paintings are blueprints of various weapons—nuclear, biological, chemical."

"No…"

She nodded again. "They have a friend who works for a defense contractor who develops these plans. He's been getting the information, and they've been working together to sell it to terrorists overseas."

"You found out what they were doing and then ran before they realized it?"

She frowned. "Not exactly. I discovered what they were doing, but the family didn't know that initially. I snuck back into the office. I actually had a double major in college—art history and computer science—so I was able to hack into their server and copy all the information on where the shipments were going. I changed the address in their system so those blueprints wouldn't get into the wrong hands."

"What happened to that information detailing their contacts?"

Her frown deepened. "I was going to give it to the FBI. However, Leo came into my office in the middle of the transfer. The jump drive flew out of my hand and into an AC vent. I had to attend a business meeting with him. While there, he got a phone call informing him that he'd been hacked. I knew he'd soon discover that I was behind it and, when he did, he'd kill me. So I left right after that meeting. I ran and I knew I couldn't look back."

"That's not Leo's story, you know."

"I can only imagine the lies he came up with."

"He said you'd gotten into a fight. That you'd been off balance and you flew off the handle. He even had a psychologist come forward and say she'd been treating you."

"They paid her to say that. I've never even been to see a counselor. That's not saying I don't need to—especially after this whole ordeal. But I've never done it."

"Tessa, did you ever go to the FBI with the information you knew?"

"I sent an anonymous tip, but apparently nothing came of it. The family is charming like that. They can talk their way out of and into almost anything. My only comfort was in knowing that I stopped one deal, at least."

Her story was so unexpected that it was a lot to comprehend, almost too much. It was going to take a while for that information to even begin to make sense. "You didn't even tell your family about any of this?"

"It all happened so fast. Besides, I knew if I was totally off the grid that Leo wouldn't even be able to threaten my family. I had to lose all contact with them, for their own safety. It was the hardest thing I've ever had to do."

Trent's heart pounded. He could imagine the choices she'd had to make. Knowing what he did only deepened his attraction to the woman. She was more than a pretty face. She also had character. "So you've been here in Gideon's Hollow?"

She nodded, her breathing more shallow than he'd like it to be. But the hike was strenuous and the cold biting. What did he expect? "I tried to isolate myself. I thought I'd done a good job... until today when you showed up."

The way her words trailed out wistfully made him wonder. But just then a light appeared in the distance. He'd save any more questions for later.

Tessa ducked behind a tree and watched carefully. Those were headlights. Was this Salem's house? His driveway?

"That's him!" she whispered. She recognized the headlights of his vintage Ford truck. That vehicle was his pride and joy.

"He's out late," Trent muttered.

"He plays bridge every Tuesday night with his friends. His wife said he doesn't usually get home until midnight. It's his splurge."

"Let's stay here a couple more minutes, just to be certain it's him. We can't be too trusting."

Tessa watched as the truck pulled to a stop in

front of the brick ranch Salem called home. A moment later, she saw him climb out and smiled. He was like a granddad to her.

The man was tall and thin and slightly hunched. He had a fringe of gray hair and a reassuring smile. Getting to know him, though she often felt as if it was a mistake, was one of the only pleasures she'd allowed herself since coming to West Virginia.

Her grin quickly vanished when she realized Salem could be in danger because of her. Whether Tessa approached him tonight or not, he could still be in a situation she'd never intended to put him in.

She'd befriended the man while working at the travel agency next door to his hardware shop. Though she'd initially tried to avoid him, it eventually had become impossible. He was always asking her how she was settling in, inviting her over for dinner, and his wife always baked cookies for her.

Just once Tessa had agreed to go eat with them, and she'd had a delightful time. It had been one of the only times since she'd moved here when she'd felt she was really a part of a community.

That realization had scared her. She'd instantly retreated back to her planned, organized and secluded life. It was for reasons just like this that she'd retreated. The people she cared for were in danger because of her.

"I don't see anyone else. I think we should go now and move quickly," Trent said.

"I hate to put him in this position," Tessa muttered, suddenly having second thoughts.

"He's already at risk, and it's not your fault. Tessa, we have little choice here, not if we want to survive. Do you understand that?"

Slowly, she nodded.

"Let's go, then." Trent took her hand again and began pulling her forward. At least his hand was warm and strong and gave her a dose of courage.

She sucked in a deep breath as they emerged from the cover of darkness. Part of her expected to feel the sting of bullets, to hear the sound of gunfire. But it was peaceful and quiet as they skirted around the gravel lane leading to the warm house in the distance.

Staying near the edge of the foliage, they rushed toward the house. By the time Tessa reached the front door, she was panting.

She glanced at Trent and got an approving nod from him before knocking. It only took a minute for the door to open.

And, to her shock, Salem stood there with a gun pointed right at them.

SIX

Trent raised his hands, fearing the worst. After everything that had happened tonight, nothing would surprise him. There was practically an all-out war being waged on Tessa.

Before he could say anything, Tessa jumped in. "I know it's late, Salem," she started. "I'm sorry if we scared you, but I had nowhere else to go."

The older man's gaze left Trent and he glanced suspiciously at Tessa. "Who's he?"

"He's…a friend," she said. "You can trust him."

"You sure?" he asked protectively.

She nodded. "Positive."

Slowly, Salem lowered his hunting rifle. He glanced behind them, scanned the background and then stepped aside. "Come on in."

A plump woman shuffled into the room, pulling her royal blue housecoat around her more closely. A heavy wrinkle formed between her eyes when she spotted everyone at the door.

"Salem? What's going on?" The woman paused

when she saw Tessa. "Tessa! What in the world are you doing here at this hour?"

"I'm sorry, Wilma." Tessa frowned, suddenly looking as though she was carrying the weight of the world on her shoulders. "I'm afraid I've put you both in a horrible situation."

"What do you mean?" Salem asked, his hands going to his hips and his perceptive eyes absorbing every motion, movement or twitch Tessa displayed—which were a lot right now. Despite the fact she was probably trying to conceal her panic, it was obvious she was a nervous wreck.

"Some men are after me. They came to my house. We got away but they found us again. I've got to get out of town. I hate to ask this, but could I borrow one of your cars?"

"Men are after you?" Salem repeated.

Tessa nodded. "It's a long story. The less you know, the better."

"Shouldn't you call the police?"

"Right now, I'm better off running."

Salem started at her another moment. "You're sure?"

She nodded again. "Unfortunately."

"Oh, Tessa." Wilma pulled her into a hug. "Why is this happening to someone as sweet as you?"

Trent knew this was an emotional moment, but time was of the essence right now. The longer they stayed here, the more likely it was they'd be discovered. But not only that, it increased the chance that someone innocent would get hurt.

Trent paced to the windows and pulled down the shades. Then he urged everyone to move toward the center of the room, just in case any bullets started flying. He had to take every precaution possible.

Tessa pulled away from Wilma's hug and glanced at Trent. "Let's just say someone very powerful wants to get revenge on me. Anyone I've had contact with is in danger." She shook her head. "I'm so sorry. I tried to keep my distance. But you both were so sweet that it was hard."

"Oh, darling," Wilma said. "You know we'd do anything for you. Of course you can use one of our cars."

Salem nodded solemnly. "I'll get the keys."

"Thank you for your help," Trent said. He switched one of the lamps off and surveyed everything outside from his position at the window. "We appreciate it."

"And who are you, exactly?" Wilma asked. Gone was her compassion and instead her shoulders rose, her eyes taking on a sharp, protective expression.

"Right now I'm her bodyguard."

Tessa's cheeks reddened. "He's someone my family trusts."

Salem returned with the keys and an envelope. "Here you go. There's some cash to hold you over."

"I couldn't possibly—" Tessa started.

"I insist."

He thrust the envelope into her hands. She looked down at it. She opened her mouth, but then closed it again as if she was speechless. "Thank you," she finally said.

"Where will you go?" Wilma asked, wringing her hands together.

Tessa glanced at Trent before shaking her head. "I have no idea."

Trent put a hand on her elbow, hating to break up the moment. He had little choice, though. "We need to move."

"We do," Tessa said, shoving the money into her pocket.

"There's one other thing," Trent started, his voice softening with compassion toward this couple who'd shown them so much kindness. "Is there anywhere the two of you could go for a few days? I fear you're in the line of fire because of your association with us."

"I couldn't stand the thought of anything happening to you," Tessa said, reaching for the older woman in front of her. The two of them stared at each other, something unspoken passing there. Compassion, understanding, concern for each other.

"We can go to stay with my sister," Wilma said. "She lives in Kentucky, and she'd be tickled to see us."

"What about the store?" Tessa asked.

"We'll put Dale in charge. You remember him? We've left him running the place before. He used to work for us full time, and he still fills in on occasion. He'll be fine while we're gone." Wilma glanced at her husband. "What do you say? It would be good to get away, right?"

Salem nodded. "It would."

"I think you should go now," Trent said. "We'll wait for you to grab a few belongings. But please hurry. There's not much time."

Trent's empathy for the couple warmed Tessa's heart. Maybe he wasn't the person she'd assumed he was when they first met. Of course, still believing he was an enemy seemed much safer than the alternative. The alternative meant her heart might feel free to explore her gut-level attraction toward the man. That possibility was crazy. The last thing she wanted was to entertain the idea of romance and love and happy-ever-after—they were all out of the reach of reality as far as she was concerned.

Salem nodded again. "Let's go grab a few

things, just enough to hold us over. I'll call Dale on the road and tell him I'm taking Wilma somewhere as a surprise."

"Good idea," Trent said, glancing out the window again. "The fewer people who know, the better."

The couple disappeared for a moment. The jitters in Tessa's stomach intensified as the impending feeling of doom continued to close in. This could get uglier before it got better—if it even got better.

Trent squeezed her shoulder and pulled her from her morbid thoughts. Electricity rushed through her with such intensity that she startled.

"You okay?" he asked.

She nodded, almost robotically. "Yeah, I guess so. As well as anyone would be in this situation."

"You're hanging in like a trouper."

"It's not even me that I'm that worried about it. It's Salem and Wilma. It's my family. There are so many other people who could be hurt because of my actions. And nothing you tell me is going to change my mind about that, so you can save your breath."

"I was going to say that I know this must be stressful for you." His gaze lingered on her, more insightful and perceptive than she would like.

Her cheeks heated. It had been a long time since her feelings were that transparent to someone. It bothered her and comforted her at the same time.

Just then, Salem and Wilma appeared with bags in hand. Tessa saw the fear in Wilma's eyes, and her guilt grew. She pulled the woman into another hug.

"Please be careful," Tessa whispered.

"I'm a tough old broad." She shrugged. "I've always wanted to say that, at least. I'll be fine. You just take care of yourself."

She gave Tessa a good motherly pat on the arm, matronly concern written across her expression.

After Tessa hugged Salem, they all went outside. Tessa made sure the couple was safely in their car before climbing in their loaner car herself. They'd been able to borrow a ten-year-old sedan. Salem liked to fix up cars in his free time, so he always seemed to have a couple of extras around.

Against her logic, she lifted up a prayer for the couple as they pulled away. *Lord, please give them safety. Cover the eyes of my attackers. Help them not to see my friends leave. Protect them.*

She opened her eyes and felt better immediately. She'd forgotten how much comfort could be found in lifting her worries up to her Creator.

Trent was staring at her as he cranked the engine. "Praying?"

She nodded reluctantly. "Desperate times call for desperate measures."

"Desperate times can teach us to depend on a higher power, even when there's no storm raging around us. That's the key we have to remember." He put the car into Drive and took off down the road.

The night was dark and Tessa kept expecting to see another car pull out behind them and another chase to begin. Thankfully, the road remained clear. She wondered how long that would be true. She wasn't naive enough to believe her troubles were over.

Trent glanced over at Tessa and saw that ever-present worry in her gaze. She was right to be so. This situation was strenuous and taxing, even for the most levelheaded person. Her concern for others—for Salem and Wilma specifically—had touched him.

All of those theories people had about her, he couldn't imagine them to be true. Obviously, she'd fled out of fear. And she was still scared. Terrified, really.

Trent had been through war zones, and this situation still felt especially intense and dangerous, much more so than he'd anticipated.

"Where are we going?" Tessa asked, wrapping her arms over her chest. Clearly, it was her way of putting up a wall, of guarding herself and protecting the little security she had left.

"I don't know yet," he answered honestly. None of this had been planned. He'd thought he'd track Tessa down, convince her to go home to her family and that would be the end of it. He'd had no idea how intricate this web of danger would be.

She remained silent a moment, her eyes fluttering back and forth in thought. "My boss has a rental house about twenty minutes away from here. I think it we could camp out there for a day or so."

"And your boss?" Trent asked. "Where will she be?"

"She's been away at a spa for the past two weeks. But she said I could use the house whenever I wanted to. Even told me what the code is to get into the lockbox where the key is located."

"Let's try that. But we'll only stay for as long as absolutely necessary—maybe one night. The longer we remain in one place, the more likely we'll be found."

"Understood."

They drove silently, except when Tessa would throw out a direction. Thankfully the road behind them remained clear, without any warnings signs of danger to come. Just where had that man gone? What was he planning next? And what had he meant when he'd said, *This woman has taken up too much of our time and energy. We need to put this behind us, and there's only one way to do that?*

There were so many questions and so few answers. He didn't want to push Tessa too hard, not right now. They'd actually made some progress in trusting each other, and he didn't want to ruin it.

The tension didn't leave him. He knew at any moment, the seemingly peaceful drive could turn dangerous. Leo's goons obviously wouldn't stop until they got what they wanted—and what they wanted was Tessa dead.

"What do you think they'll do next?" she muttered, staring straight ahead. "How would you track someone down if you were on their side?"

That was a great question, but it was complicated. He let out a deep breath. "Considering the fact that I believe they followed me here, I think they're probably looking into your life in Gideon's Hollow now. I assume they left someone to keep watch over your house to see if you go back. They'll think of ways to talk to anyone you had contact with and look for any indications as to where you might run."

"What about my boss, Chris? Do you think they'll look for us at her place?"

"It's a risk we have to take right now. I'm hoping we're far enough ahead of them that they won't catch up yet."

"I see."

"If you left any emails on your computer, they'll examine those. They'll try to access your phone records."

"So how much time do we have?" She almost sounded resigned as she asked the question.

"Maybe a couple of days."

"It sounds as if we—I—need to go somewhere totally off the radar."

He stole a glance at her, trying to gauge her emotions. As the moonlight hit her profile, he sucked in a breath. Man, was she beautiful— take-his-breath-away beautiful. "You don't think I'm going to leave you alone, do you?"

"As far as I'm concerned, we're not in this together. You should go back and tell my family that you weren't successful. Maybe just tell them that I'm most likely dead. Whatever it takes to ease their pain. I'm assuming the not knowing is probably the hardest part for them."

"I led these men to you, Tessa. This is partly my fault. I can't abandon you." Leo must have been tracking his moves. Especially if it was like Tessa had said—the man had pretended to be a friend to her family when all along he was behind everything. The realization had solidified in his mind the longer he thought about it. That meant it was partly Trent's fault that Tessa was in her current situation.

"I don't want you to feel obligated. This is my problem, not yours. You should get out now while you can."

He couldn't imagine leaving her behind at a time like this. It wasn't even that he felt obligated—there was just some part of him that knew he couldn't abandon her now. The girl would be a sitting duck. Besides, no one should be terrified and alone.

He intended on sticking with her until this was resolved. He had a feeling her life depended on it. And, by default, so did his.

Tessa hated to admit it, but she felt grateful for Trent's steadfastness. Most people would have jumped ship at the first opportunity. But Trent was here and, even if she wanted to get rid of him, she wasn't sure she'd be able to. His presence comforted her, as did his size and skills. He'd proved himself to be more than capable.

But reality still haunted her. Leo's men had found her. If they went through her emails, they'd find correspondence with Chris, her boss at the travel agency. Thankfully, Salem didn't believe in email, so maybe those men wouldn't connect Tessa with the hardware-store owner and his wife.

Salem and Wilma were now out of town. Chris was also out of the area. Tessa could only pray they'd remain safe. They seemed to be the most at risk.

"Chris's cabin should be down this road," she said, her voice sounding more like a croak.

Trent turned down a narrow road. At the end of the street, a house appeared. Even in the dark, Tessa could see a gentle stream rippling behind the property. Trent pulled around behind the structure and cut the engine. "So we rest up and then we hit the road again in the morning. Sound good?"

Tessa nodded, overwhelmed by the task ahead of her. Was there anywhere she'd be safe? She typed in the code on the lockbox by the front door and found the spare key inside. They unlocked the door and stepped inside, hitting the light switch on the wall. A cozy cabin came into view.

Her throat tightened at the thought of staying here with Trent. It wasn't ideal. But what other choice did they have? At least the place was large enough that one of them could stay upstairs and the other downstairs. And she'd sleep with her door locked. She wouldn't take any chances, despite his dedication so far. One could never be too careful.

"We'll take off in the morning," Trent said, turning toward her.

As she glanced up at him and realized how close they were standing, heat rushed to her cheeks. She'd known he was handsome. But standing here in the light right now, there was no denying that the man was attractive.

She swallowed hard and took a step back, surprised at how appealing he seemed at the moment. "That sounds good. I'll stay upstairs."

He nodded, his eyes still on her as if he was trying to figure her out. He'd obviously noticed the change in her, seen the flash of embarrassment in her eyes. "Good night, then."

Before either of them could take a step away, a sound outside caught their ears.

Tessa saw Trent tense also, then he grabbed her arm, cut the lights and pulled her against the wall. Her senses came alive as adrenaline pumped through her.

No way had those men tracked her down already…had they?

Then they heard the sound again. It was clearly a car. Pulling down the lane. Coming toward the cabin.

SEVEN

Trent knew something wasn't right. No way would these guys pull up to a cabin in the middle of the night and practically announce their arrival. They were more cunning than that.

So who was here?

He peered out the window, saw a sedan pull up and the headlights go dark. Then a woman stepped out.

"Blonde, heavyset, midfifties."

Tessa visible relaxed beside him. "Chris. That must be Chris. But she wasn't supposed to be back for another week."

"Come on. We don't want to scare her." Trent pulled her away from the wall and opened the door just as Chris stepped onto the porch.

The woman gasped in surprise. "You scared the living daylights out of me!" Then her gaze fell on Tessa. "Tessa? What are you doing here?"

"I didn't mean to scare you. You said I could

use the cabin whenever I wanted, and I thought you were at a spa."

Chris's eyes went to Trent, and she gave him a knowing look. "I see."

Tessa shook her head, her cheeks reddening. "No, it's not like that. It's actually a really long story. I just needed some place to go because of some problems at my own cabin. Like I said, I didn't expect you to be here."

"I decided to end my vacation a little early and have some downtime here at my mountain retreat." She held her flowered luggage up a little higher.

"We can leave," Tessa said, apology in her tone.

Trent wondered if Tessa realized exactly what she was saying, because they had nowhere else to go.

"No, no." Chris waved a hand in the air, suddenly acting as if this wasn't a big deal. "Please stay. Just let me get inside and put my stuff down."

"Of course." Tessa stepped aside, offering a fleeting glance toward Trent.

Trent could tell she felt awkward. Anyone would in her situation, and his heart twisted with a moment of compassion. Usually when he got focused on a task, he tried to clear away any emotions in favor of logic. Logic could help keep them alive.

But at the moment Tessa seemed so alone. There was something deeper inside Trent, something he couldn't exactly pinpoint, that kept him here. It wasn't an obligation. It wasn't duty.

It was purpose, he realized. It was no accident he was here to help. He believed God had ordained the timing.

Chris pushed past them and deposited everything inside the door before flipping on the lights. Once they were all inside and the door closed, she turned to them. "Anyone care to explain?"

Tessa cast another glance at Trent, and he could tell she was struggling to find the right words. He decided to step in. "Someone broke into Tessa's place, and she needed to go somewhere else for the night."

Chris eyed him suspiciously. "And you are?"

"I'm just a family friend who came to visit."

"I thought you didn't have any family," Chris said, turning back to Tessa.

Tessa laughed nervously. "I mean, everyone has family, even if there are some members you'd like to forget. Besides, he's a family *friend*."

"Well, I'm sorry to hear about your home," Chris said, accepting her answer. She walked into the kitchen and fixed a glass of water, taking a long sip before clanking the glass on the counter. "That must have been scary, and I'm glad I can be of help. You're welcome to stay here. There's one bedroom upstairs and I usually stay down here."

"I'll take the couch," Trent offered.

"Very well, then. I'm exhausted, so I'm going to turn in. I'll see you both in the morning."

She grabbed her things and shuffled off to the bedroom, shutting the door behind her. A moment later, the lock clicked in place.

"Thanks for covering for me," Tessa whispered, stepping closer and glancing toward Chris's closed door. "My mind went blank."

"It's not a problem."

She nodded upstairs and let out a deep sigh. "I'm going to turn in. I know we have a long day ahead. Good night."

His gaze lingered on her as she disappeared upstairs. She really was lovely. He'd known that even before he met her. But there was something about her that made it hard to pull his eyes away. Maybe it was the way her glossy hair swept over her shoulders. The way she nibbled on her lip when she got nervous. How her eyes told the story of what was going on in her head and heart.

When Tessa disappeared from sight, Trent pulled out his cell. Could they be tracking him through his phone? Was that how they'd found him here?

It was an idea he definitely needed to consider.

But right now he needed to call for help. When he finished this conversation, he'd ditch his phone, just to be on the safe side.

He dialed one of his old friends from the police academy, Zach Davis. The two had started on the force together in Richmond, Virginia. Later, Zach had moved up to Baltimore and then to a little island on the Chesapeake Bay. The bonds they'd forged through the academy had never faded, though. Trent knew Zach had a few weeks off before starting a new job as sheriff, so he would be the perfect person to help.

Zach answered before the second ring, his voice scratchy but alert. "Trent?"

"Sorry to wake you." Trent paced to the far side of the house and lowered his voice so no one would hear. The situation would be tricky because Leo McAllister was a man with connections. Plus, even though he'd chided Tessa for her trust issues, he had some himself.

The police had investigated Leo after Tessa had disappeared, but they'd found no evidence of wrongdoing. It didn't help either that no one, not even law enforcement, wanted to mess with the McAllister family. They were powerful, made big donations to charities, including the Fraternal Order of Police, and they had the ear of senators and other legislative leaders.

If Trent was wrong about Leo—if Tessa wasn't telling the truth, for some reason—then they'd be opening a can of worms that was best left untouched. That was why Trent knew there were only two people he could trust—Zach and their mutual friend Gabe Michaels.

For all he knew, the McAllisters could have men in the local police or even with the FBI. They were rich enough to buy anyone willing to sell themselves for a price.

"What time is it?" Zach asked, his voice groggy.

He glanced at clock in the distance. "Three thirty."

"I'm assuming this is important."

"Life or death. There's no one else I can trust. I need you to look into someone for me. His name is Leo McAllister."

"Okay…"

"He may have ties with terrorists."

"Sounds serious."

"I did mention life or death. However, this could go a lot deeper than just my life." Tessa entered his mind. But this was also greater than even her life. If what Tessa had told him was true—and he had no reason to believe it wasn't—then the lives of a lot of Americans could be at stake. A terrorist cell developing weapons was huge.

Trent filled Zach in on the other details about Leo that he knew.

"I'll see what I can find out and get back to you."

"There's no time to waste on this, Zach," Trent said. "You should be careful, too. If you try to breach their computer system, they'll be alerted. It's important to circumvent anything you do on the web."

"I'll start now," Zach said. "And I'll be cautious."

Trent only hoped he wasn't already too late.

Tessa couldn't relax. She'd forced herself to lie in bed, but she'd left all of her clothes on, even her shoes. Instead of crawling under the covers, she'd lain on top of them and pulled a spare blanket over her legs in order to stay warm. She felt better being dressed and ready to run if necessary.

Just one more rule of survival: always be prepared.

Her body was tired, but her adrenaline made it hard for her to sleep. She lay in bed, staring at the ceiling, replaying everything and fretting about what the future would hold.

What would it be like to believe that God was in control? That whatever happened, He could work it for good? Right now, she needed some hope and comfort. Relying on herself—even relying on Trent—just didn't seem like enough. It was going to take a force greater than the two of them in order to survive this.

She'd gone to church growing up, so she knew the scriptures. She just felt as if God had been silent in her life for the past year. Or was she the one who'd stopped talking?

When Tessa really thought about it, she realized her relationship with God had dwindled before all of this had happened with Leo. In college, she'd drifted away from her beliefs. She'd considered herself a Christian in name, but she hadn't lived like someone who followed Christ. No, she'd let worldly lures take hold in her life. She'd enjoyed the finer things—designer clothes, pampering herself, making her career her number one priority.

Leo had fit right in with that side of her. She'd loved the luxuries he'd provided; she'd even reveled in them. But looking back, she'd felt hollow inside during that time. All of those things hadn't brought her the satisfaction she'd hoped for. All it had done was to leave her wanting more and more.

When she'd gone on the run and everything had been stripped away, Tessa had to come to terms with who she was as a person, without the fancy clothes or perfect hair or admirable career.

She hadn't liked the image that stared back at

her. Her changes had happened so slowly that she hadn't even realized they'd taken effect. Sin was like that: people could dip a toe in and before they knew it be fully immersed.

But those were things she'd think about later. Her thoughts turned to Trent. Despite her doubts, he'd been kind. He could have left her in the middle of the craziness, like most sensible people would have. But he'd stuck by her, even risking his life.

Her family trusted him. Maybe she could, too.

As she turned over in bed again, unable to sleep, her mind drifted from Trent to Chris. Why had her boss had such a strange reaction to her? Of course it was strange that Chris had found her here. Tessa couldn't deny that. But there was more to it.

Did Chris think that Tessa was up to no good? That almost seemed to match her reaction.

She and her boss had always had a peculiar relationship. Chris didn't really need to work or generate income. Her late husband had left her with a lot of money, enough to own three houses and take vacations whenever she wanted. But the woman liked traveling so much that she'd decided to open her own travel agency in town. They hardly ever had any clients. Tessa hadn't complained because the job helped her to pay the bills and the lackluster business kept her isolated.

Chris was in and out, though—more out than in. She basically trusted Tessa to run the business from the little storefront in downtown Gideon's Hollow. It was a nice, quiet job with very little interaction with those in town—ideal for Tessa.

Now she wondered if Chris had bought Trent's story. He'd told the truth. But Tessa knew that despite their best efforts, they'd been acting suspiciously. She'd never been a good liar. Even though Trent had sounded calm, one look at Tessa and Chris would have known that something was off.

She wished she could stop fretting about it, though.

As she started to drift off to sleep, she heard something downstairs. Just as she jolted upright in bed, her door flung open.

"Freeze! Put your hands up!" A police officer stood there, his gun drawn and aimed at her.

Trent kept his hands raised in the air, his gaze quickly surveying the men around him. Five men had burst into the house from both the front and back doors. They wore SWAT gear with helmets and carried military-grade weapons.

He'd taken one look and known he had no chance of taking them all down. So he'd risen from the couch and tried to keep his cool instead. But his thoughts clashed inside his head.

How had these men, whoever they were, found them here? He had his suspicions.

Chris had stepped out of her bedroom fifteen minutes ago, said she needed some air, and five minutes after she returned the men had invaded the house.

At the moment, Chris appeared unbothered. She stood by the front door with her arms crossed and a look of worry on her face. She'd been the one who led these men here. But why would she do something like this? What would her motive be?

A moment later, Trent saw one of the officers leading Tessa downstairs. Her arms were raised also, and terror stained her eyes. Anyone would be scared in this situation. Her gaze met his and he saw the questions there. He wished he had answers to give her.

A man—the one who appeared to be in charge—strutted up to Trent and got in his face. The man stared wordlessly, waiting for Trent to flinch, to break his gaze. Trent refused.

When he got no reaction from Trent, the man took a step back and glowered. "Arrest both of them."

"On what count?" Trent asked.

"Conspiring with terrorists, for starters."

"What evidence could possibly prove that?" None. There was no way they had any proof.

"Tessa has been on our watch list for quite a while. Unfortunately, you've proved to be her accomplice," the man continued. "We take threats like this very seriously."

This wasn't making any sense, not by any stretch of the imagination. "What agency are you with?"

"The West Virginia State Police. We're bringing you in, but I'm sure the FBI will want a piece of you, also. You two have a lot of explaining to do."

Something still wasn't settling right in his gut. There were six men altogether and four had guns trained on Trent and Tessa. There was little he could do at his point.

One of the men pulled Trent's hands down and cuffed him. Another officer did the same for Tessa.

"You have the right to remain silent," the officer started.

Tessa struggled against the man. It was just the distraction he needed. As the man in front of him looked away, Trent reached back and grabbed an upholstery tack from the breakfast bar. Chris must have been re-covering one of her chairs. Working carefully, subtly, Trent pressed two tacks into his leather belt, praying no one would notice.

Just as he secured the second tack, his captor jerked his arms back and began leading him outside.

Tessa swung her head toward Chris as she passed.

"You did this, didn't you?" Hurt and betrayal were evident in her voice.

The woman shook her head, sorrow in her eyes. "I was already on my way home when they called me a few hours ago and told me what you'd been up to. I had to do my part to help. I always thought your background sounded kind of suspicious, Tessa. I just never imagined you were capable of this."

"I'm not. I'm not guilty of anything here," Tessa said, squirming as the office behind her shoved her forward. "Chris, you have no idea what you've done…"

The woman raised her chin. "I'm just being a patriot."

With another rough shove, the officer pushed Trent outside to a police cruiser. His eyes soaked in the unmarked car. It must have pulled up after the men got inside the house. Otherwise, Trent would have heard the car approach. After all, he hadn't gotten a wink of sleep. His mind was too busy turning over things.

He glanced around. Four men still had their

guns in hand, ready to use. And Trent was hand-cuffed. This was no time to make a move or try to escape, especially if it meant that Tessa would be in the line of fire.

Right before he was escorted into the backseat of the cruiser, he let one of the tacks drop from his hands. With any luck, the tip would pierce the tire and maybe buy them some more time.

Thankfully, Tessa tumbled into the backseat beside him. He'd prayed they wouldn't be separated, because that would only make things more complicated.

The door slammed shut but no officers climbed in. They stayed outside in the lingering darkness, talking quietly among themselves. Chris stood on the porch, watching everything with her arms crossed and a look of both anxiety and pride across her face.

"I'm scared, Trent," Tessa whispered.

"You should be."

"Do you think they'll let us go if I tell them the whole story?" Her voice trembled.

He wanted to say, to do something to comfort her. But he had to tell her the truth. "Tessa, these men aren't the police."

Her eyes widened. "Then who are they?"

"My guess? They're men your ex-fiancé sent."

EIGHT

Tessa felt as though she might pass out. She'd thought she'd been anxious before, but what she experienced now was beyond any of her earlier apprehensions. She was downright panicky, to the point of fearing she might hyperventilate.

"What do you mean?" she whispered. "They had uniforms on."

"You can buy anything online. SWAT uniforms, fake badges. You name it."

A shiver raced through her and didn't cease. Her body continued to tremble and cold washed over her. "They're going to kill us."

"Listen, don't let on that you know anything. Okay? We'll figure a way out together. But we need to play it cool."

"So you have a plan?" She desperately hoped he did.

"Considering I have no idea what's going to happen, it's really hard to create a firm strategy of how to escape. So I'll do the next best thing."

"What's that?"

"I'll wait for the right opportunity."

"Here they come," she whispered.

Two men climbed into the front seat. The other four climbed into another cruiser. Tessa cast one more glance at Chris as they pulled away. How could her friend think that she was guilty? Didn't she know her any better?

Of course, Leo could be convincing. He could talk the most intelligent person into believing whatever lies he wanted to sell. Besides, if there really had been something suspicious, it *was* Chris's duty to report it. The woman had no idea the web of deceit that had been spun around her.

Okay, God, I'm listening. Maybe that's been the problem. It's not that You've been silent. It's that I haven't been ready to hear. I'm ready now. I'm sorry that it's taken this moment of absolute desperation to get me to this point.

The sun started to peek over the mountains as they headed east. Tessa assumed that meant it was probably approaching seven. The sun was coming up later now that it was getting cooler outside.

She tried to focus on the things she knew. The definites were more comforting than the uncertainties. That was why she watched the landscape out the window as they passed. That was why she concentrated on the sunrise. Why she listened to the men's voices in the front seat as they muttered quietly to each other. Glass separated them and she couldn't make out their words. But they definitely didn't have West Virginia accents. Trent was right.

She glanced at him then. She could see from the look in his eyes that he was mulling the situation over and running through possibilities. As strange as it might seem, she was glad he was here with her. Even though the situation felt practically hopeless, he was the reason she had a small grain of hope that they'd survive. Alone, she'd be dead by now.

He caught her looking at him and sent her a questioning look. "You okay?"

She shrugged. "Depends on how you define *okay*. I'm sure you're regretting taking this assignment, huh?"

"No, not at all."

"You could die because of it."

He leaned closer, close enough that she could feel his breath on her cheek. "Tessa, if what you've told me is true, this family needs to be exposed. I'm going to do everything I can to fight for justice."

Something welled in her—she wasn't sure what. Pride? Gratitude? He had the heart of a soldier, of a fighter, and she could appreciate that. The world needed people who weren't afraid to battle for what they believed in, to fight for the rights of others.

She wished she had some of that same resolve. Maybe she wouldn't be in this situation. Maybe she wouldn't have retreated in the first place.

Suddenly, the car lurched. It jerked to the right so hard that Tessa tumbled into Trent. Had one of the tires been shot out?

As the car pulled over to a stop on the side of the road, Tessa held her breath and waited to see what would happen next.

Was this the moment of opportunity Trent had mentioned?

"Stay here," the driver said gruffly.

Trent watched every move the bogus police officers made. It appeared the tack he'd thrown down had finally wedged itself into the tire and led to a blowout. Thankfully, the other car had gone ahead of them. That meant that it was just Trent, Tessa and the two men escorting them. However, Trent and Tessa were at a disadvantage because of their handcuffs. But hopefully that wouldn't be a problem for long. He'd been subtly trying to work the second tack he'd pressed into his belt into the lock mechanism of the handcuffs.

Finally, he heard a soft click. He'd done it.

Now he had to figure out how to reach Tessa without drawing any attention to the fact.

The driver jerked the door open. "You're going to have to get out while we change the tire."

He grabbed Tessa first and dragged her outside. Before the man could reach for Trent, he scooted from the car, making sure his handcuffs stayed in place for the time being.

"Guard them while I change this," the driver mumbled to his partner.

The other man—the slighter of the two—aimed his gun at Trent and Tessa. He appeared youngish—maybe in his midtwenties, and he was both scrawny and obviously outranked in this merry little group of bandits. The driver had called him Grath once.

"Stay over there," Grath said. "Don't make a move or you're dead."

"We're dead anyway, aren't we?" Trent said.

A gleam appeared in the man's eyes, and he nodded toward Tessa. "Not until the big man sees her. He wants to handle this personally."

That must be Leo. He wanted to make sure Tessa suffered. Trent didn't like the sound of that.

Immediately, visions of Laurel appeared in his mind. He couldn't let that happen again. Laurel had been his whole world and made him feel like the luckiest man alive. Sure, they'd had their problems. But they'd been happy together.

Until one of his supposed friends had stabbed

him in the back. He'd been tasked with guarding Laurel while Trent was testifying in court.

The gang he was trying put away had threatened Trent's life if he proceeded with his investigation. He'd known Laurel would be in danger, as well. That was why he'd taken the extra precautions to keep her safe. He didn't want to be bullied.

But then one of his own friends, Richard, had been bought off. Richard hadn't pulled the trigger on Laurel himself, but he'd taken money and given away her location to men who'd been bent on revenge toward Trent. Those men had shot Richard in the shoulder, an injury that looked more serious than it was. Then those thugs had killed Laurel.

His friend had denied his involvement for weeks—months. But Trent had begun to trail him. He'd caught him meeting with a gang member. A check of his bank account had proved Richard had been paid off. When he'd brought the evidence to his colleagues, they hadn't taken him seriously. They'd thought he was obsessed and desperate to find someone to take the blame.

That was when Trent had left the police department and struck out on his own. Eventually, he'd taken his evidence all the way to the top and gotten some results. He'd pressed charges and Richard had gone to jail. But the whole thing had left Trent disillusioned.

He wasn't going to let the same thing happen to Tessa that had happened to Laurel.

Moving quietly, wordlessly, Trent slipped the tack into Tessa's hands. She felt it for a moment before looking up at him with confusion.

Subtly, he motioned toward his handcuffs. Her eyes widened with understanding and she nodded.

As Grath looked away for a brief second, Trent swung his leg through the air. His foot connected with the man's gun and sent it toppling to the ground. In that moment, the driver reached for his own gun and aimed it at Trent.

In a flash, Trent grabbed Grath and pulled the man in front of him to use as a human shield. The driver discharged his gun, and Grath let out a groan as the bullet hit his shoulder.

Before the driver had a chance to realize what was happening, Trent shoved Grath on top of him. The action afforded Trent enough time to grab the driver's gun.

The two struggled with the weapon. In a battle of strength, the barrel of the gun volleyed back and forth from the driver to Trent.

Despite the chill in the air, sweat sprinkled across Trent's forehead. The man was tougher than he'd given him credit for. Their struggle continued in what felt like slow motion.

"Give it up," the driver mumbled, his face red with exertion.

"Never." Trent used all the strength in him to aim the gun back toward the driver.

Both men grunted, bared their teeth. Their lives were on the line. Whoever was the strongest would live.

That man had to be Trent.

Suddenly, a gunshot filled the air. The driver let out a howl of pain. Trent's eyes traveled to the man's shoulder. A spot of blood grew there.

Trent jerked his eyes behind him. Tessa stood there, gun in hand. She looked shell-shocked, but okay.

She might have just saved his life.

With half of her handcuffs still around her wrist, she tucked the gun into her waistband and hurried toward Trent. "Are you okay?"

He took a step back from the driver, who was still alive but moaning with pain. "Yeah, I'm fine. We need to go."

"I'll get the tire. You move these guys out of the way?"

Trent stared at her a moment, unsure he'd heard her correctly. But she was already at the tire, unscrewing the lug nuts. "Got it."

He grabbed the driver and pulled him off to

the side of the road. The man would be okay. His partners would come back to check on these two when they realized they were no longer responding. Grath would also be okay. He'd been hit in the shoulder, but it wasn't life threatening.

That meant it was even more urgent that Trent and Tessa got out of there fast.

"They'll…find…you," the driver muttered, teeth bared.

"We're going to make that as hard as possible," Trent said, patting the man's cheek. He reached into his pocket and grabbed the man's phone. Then he snatched the extra gun and some cash. He and Tessa were going to need whatever they could get in order to survive this.

He got back to Tessa in time to help her slip the new tire on. "A girl who knows her way around a car. Impressive."

"My dad insisted I know how to take care of myself."

"It's really paying off now," Trent said, helping her finish. "Come on. Let's go."

She climbed into the passenger seat as he slammed the driver's door shut. He cranked the engine and started down the road, his heart pounding as he realized what'd just happened. That could have turned out so much differently.

Thank You, Lord.

"We don't have much time," Trent said.

"What do you mean? You think those other guys will find us?" Tessa glanced back, as if expecting to see the second car. Then she began fiddling with the handcuff still left on one wrist. She unlatched it and stuck the tack into her pocket.

"Unfortunately, I fear they'll find us sooner rather than later. This car probably has a GPS and they'll be able to track us down."

"So what do we do?"

"We hold tight for a little while. As soon as we're able to, we'll ditch this car and get a new one."

"That sounds easier said than done." She shivered and stared out the window a moment, a certain melancholy washing over her. "You think those guys will be okay?"

He nodded. "They'll be fine."

"That's the first time I've ever shot someone."

"You saved my life." He glanced over and saw the worry across her features. He reached across the seat and squeezed her hand. "You were brave. You did the right thing. Those guys were ruthless, Tessa. There's no telling what would have happened when we got to whatever destination they were taking us to."

She nodded uncertainly. "Mentally, I know that. Emotionally, I'm still spinning."

He squeezed again before pulling his hand back to his side. "I know it's tough."

She drew in a deep breath. "I have to stop thinking about that. I've got to start focusing on survival."

With that, she opened the glove compartment.

Tessa riffled through the papers that had been left in the car. Certainly there was some information here, even if it was fake.

"What are you doing?" Trent asked her.

"I'm seeing if I can find anything useful," Tessa told him. "Maybe there's some evidence of what they were planning. Whatever information we can arm ourselves with, the better."

"I agree."

Tessa thought she saw a touch of admiration in his eyes. She continued to browse the papers, but saw nothing helpful. The car was registered to someone named John Tracy. The name didn't ring any bells with Tessa. Some sales papers indicated it had been purchased in Alexandria, Virginia. It couldn't be a coincidence.

Tessa had worked in a gallery outside Washington, DC, just a few miles from Alexandria. That was where Leo had based all his operations. This only solidified everything in her mind. Leo had hired these men and sent them after her.

How many were out there, searching for them? Right now, it almost seemed like an unending army. There'd been the men at her cabin who'd driven off the cliff. The ones at Trent's cabins who'd followed them through the woods. Then this group. How many would Tessa have to defeat before she'd won the battle?

Tessa knew that someone with Leo's power, money and influence could afford to hire as many people as he wanted. He'd made millions on his arms trade. She'd sneaked onto his computer and seen the numbers herself.

What she'd never been able to figure out was his motive. Was it just the money? Did he really hate this country that much? Maybe it was both. Maybe it was just to carry out his family's legacy. Until eight months ago when she'd made her discoveries, Tessa had never had any indication that he had ties to terrorists.

After that, she'd been able to put some of the facts into place. Leo did have a lot of hushed phone calls and out-of-town business trips. She'd always thought it was because he was trying to secure new art deals.

Suddenly, something landed in her lap. She looked down and saw a wallet. "What's this?"

"I took it from the man driving the car. See what's inside."

She opened the bifold and saw at least six one-hundred-dollar bills. The man's driver's license read Tom Tracy and he was from Wilmington Heights. His picture seemed to glare at her from the plastic identification card.

She continued to go through the wallet and found two credit cards, a slip of paper with an address on it and a season pass to a local amusement park.

Funny, even men like John Tracy had a life outside criminal activities.

"Anything?"

She held up the paper. "An address."

"What is it?"

"It's in Wilmington Heights, Virginia. 123 Arnold Drive."

He handed her a phone. "This also belongs to one of the men who were after us. Look up the address on the map. I'm guessing it's near DC. Within an hour, at least."

"You think it's where they were going to take us?"

"It's my best guess."

Before she could pull up the map, the phone beeped. An incoming call.

A name popped up on the screen.

Leo McAllister.

NINE

Trent stared at the phone a moment, contemplating his options and weighing the possible consequences. He didn't have much time to make up his mind.

"What should I do?" Tessa asked. "If no one answers, Leo will get suspicious."

Trent held out his hand, decision made. "Let me have the phone."

Her eyes widened even more. "Are you…?"

He nodded.

After a moment of hesitation, she slipped the device into his hands. He drew in a deep breath before putting it to his ear and answering. "Hello."

"Tom, what's the word?" a deep voice asked.

Trent kept his voice neutral, trying to sound indistinguishable. "So far, so good."

"You running on schedule still?"

"By all calculations, yes."

"How's the girl?"

"Scared."

"Good. Wait till she sees me." He let out a diabolical yet untethered laugh.

Trent forced himself to let out a deep chuckle, also. He had to sound as if he was on Leo's side, even if the mere thought of it made him feel sick to his stomach. "Yes, sir."

"All right. See you in a few hours, then."

Trent hung up and glanced at Tessa. Again, his heart welled with compassion and protectiveness. Leo was planning something extremely painful as a repercussion for her betraying him. Trent couldn't let that happen. Anger surged through him at the thought. How people could be that twisted, that selfish, that evil was hard to fathom. Yet he'd seen his fair share of evil. He'd fought terrorists before. He'd won. He was determined to do the same here with Tessa.

"Well?"

"He says he'll see us in a few hours. Wherever they were going, it wasn't terribly far away." DC was probably three hours from here, but the suburbs could be reached in two or less.

"So what do we do?"

"Call the number on the back of those credit cards. See if we can find out how much is left on the credit line. We're going to need a new vehicle." He glanced at the dashboard. "And gas."

With trembling hands, she began making the calls. "It looks as if there's about five thousand," she said several minutes later. "You think we can get away with using these?"

"If we find a small dealer and we go at dusk so we're less recognizable. Or if I put a hat on to disguise my face a little more. There are a lot of factors here." They'd all raced through his mind at once, causing a small throb to start forming at the back of his head. There was so much at stake. One wrong move could end with both of them dead.

Not on his watch.

"Okay. Whatever we have to do."

"It's not ideal," he said. "But there aren't a lot of choices."

"You're right. If we are where I think, there's a town about fifteen minutes from here. It's small, but large enough to have a variety of businesses. Maybe we can find something there."

"Even better—look up some online ads." Buying from a private dealer was the best option. He prayed that everything would fall into place.

Tessa got busy, her fingers flying across the phone's keyboard and her gaze concentrated on the screen. "This one looks promising."

"Call them."

Tessa did as he asked. When she hung up, she said, "The seller said we can go to his house now. He has one of those credit card readers, so he'll let us use our cards."

"Perfect. Tell me how to get there."

Ten minutes later, they pulled up to a small house in the mountains. A man named Jim with long hair pulled back into a ponytail met them outside and showed them a faded red sedan he was selling.

"If I'd had more time, I would have cleaned it up for you. It's a little junky inside. My apologies," Jim said in a West Virginia drawl.

Trent peered inside and saw some old soda cans in the backseat, along with some napkins and a few magazines. That wasn't what concerned him. He really needed to see under the hood.

Jim popped it open for him and Trent examined the hoses and belts, checked the fluids and looked for any corrosion. Afterward, he cranked the engine and listened to it run for a moment.

"You two from around here?" Jim asked, crossing his arms and looking as if he had all the time in the world.

"Not too far away," Trent said. "We've been looking for a new car for the family. We didn't want to let this one pass us by."

The man tapped his knuckles on the side of the vehicle. "She may not be beautiful, but she's solid. I fixed her up myself. It's what I do—find oysters and make them into pearls and then I sell them."

Trent didn't have enough time to make all of

this small talk. He stepped from the driver's seat and held out his hand. "We'll take it."

A smile spread across the man's face and he closed the deal with a handshake. "Sounds great. Let me go get my phone and card reader."

As he hurried into his house, Tessa looked up at Trent. "You think this can get us out of town?"

"The car seems to run well, even if it is junky. And the price is right. Now we just have to hope this payment goes through."

Jim returned with his smartphone. Trent's fingers were steady as he handed the credit card to him.

Jim looked at the card for a moment and then back at Trent. "Since this is such a large transaction, could I see some ID, also?"

"Of course." He reached back into the wallet and emerged with the driver's license. He tugged at his hat as Jim studied the picture a moment. The man looked at the image there and then back at Trent.

Trent held his breath, waiting for Jim's conclusion. This could ruin everything for Trent and Tessa. He only prayed Jim didn't look too closely.

"These pictures really make us look horrible, don't they?" Jim finally said with a laugh.

A chuckled escaped from Trent as he let out the breath he held. "You're telling me. Or maybe it's the fact I need bifocals but keep resisting. I don't feel old enough for that yet."

"Let me get this done." He swiped the card, waited a moment and then looked up with a smile. "All set."

"Perfect."

Jim handed him his card back, along with the car keys and title. "Enjoy!"

Trent glanced at Tessa, and she nodded. She took the keys from him. "I'll be driving this. I'll see you later...honey."

"I'll see you at home," Trent said, just as they'd rehearsed.

They'd discussed abandoning the fake police cruiser a little farther down the road, hopping into the sedan and taking off.

Trent had walked four steps toward the cruiser when Jim called his name. His fake name. Had Jim realized what they were up to? Trent prayed that wasn't the case.

Trent froze, his skin pricking. He turned around, plastering on a fake smile. "Yes?"

Jim held out a bag of apples. "Here, take these. I have several trees on my property, so I like to give them away to everyone I can. No way I can eat all of them."

Trent slowly let out his breath. "Thank you."

He took the apples and smiled as he turned away.

* * *

"The town is about five miles from here. We're going to need to stop for some gas," Tessa said.

Just then, her stomach let out a grumble.

Trent tossed her an apple. "See if this will hold you over. We'll need get something to eat soon, too. Our energy will run out before our adrenaline."

"I could use a quick bite."

"We'll get it to go. We're not far enough away to feel comfortable."

Tessa shrugged her shoulders back. "I just can't relax. It's as if I'm waiting for a deer to pop out in the middle of the road at any minute. Only it's not an innocent deer. It's worse. But then I think—how would these guys know where we are?"

"They're pretty smart, so I'm not putting anything past them. Soon they'll realize that the two henchmen we left on the side of the road aren't answering their phone. They'll check things out. The men will be found on the road, taken to a hospital and they'll check in with Leo. We're basically on borrowed time here."

She shuddered again. "It almost feels like a no-win situation."

"It's not. You've handled yourself well so far. Your work with the gun was impressive, to say the least."

"All those lessons are paying off, I guess."

"I'd say so."

A few minutes later, a little town came into view. It looked like a classic mountain community with one main street filled with old buildings that could use some renovation. Still, the storefronts served the purpose they were needed for. There was a post office, a convenience store, a hardware store, deli and gas station.

While Trent got gas, Tessa hurried inside and cleaned herself up in the bathroom. She eyed the deli right beside the gas station, her mouth watering at the thought of a nice warm sandwich. Instead, she opted to grab some of the premade ones at the gas station, along with some bottles of water, crackers and a prepaid cell phone. She feared Leo would trace the one they used earlier, so they'd left it in the abandoned car.

She paid using the cash Salem had given her. She'd had to leave her backpack at Chris's, but at least she had this money, as well as what Trent had taken from the man who'd abducted them. She'd also kept Grath's gun, just in case.

One day, she'd repay Salem for all of his kindness. She had a lot of people to repay, for that matter. At the top of her list was Trent.

As Tessa left the store, she froze in her tracks.

Emerging from the deli were the four other men who'd been at Chris's place. They'd ditched their fake police uniforms and had fountain drinks in hand, talking merrily as if they were just some friends out for a good time.

She had to get Trent and get out of here.

Now.

TEN

Seeing the alarm across Tessa's face, Trent followed her gaze and spotted the men from the other SUV. He instantly turned around before they recognized his face. Tessa dropped behind a gas pump and pretended to tie her shoe.

Their gazes connected and no words were needed. This was a very precarious situation, and one wrong move would throw their entire plan into upheaval.

From where Trent stood, he could hear a phone ring. One of the men answered.

"What do you mean he's not picking up?" the man barked. "They were right behind us."

Trent motioned for Tessa to hop in the car. Remaining low, she climbed into the front seat and sank down. Trent finished pumping gas and screwed the lid back on the tank. He moved at a normal pace, remaining casual but keeping his back toward the men near him.

"We'll go check it out and make sure nothing

happened," the man continued. "We know how important this is to you. You want the girl. Alive. Or, at least, alive enough that you can deal with her yourself."

A glance from the corner of Trent's eye showed that the men were creeping closer, walking toward their vehicle, which must have been parked out of sight on the other side of the station.

One of them glanced his way as he passed. Trent tugged his hat down lower. He had to keep a cool head.

Something seemed to register in the man's gaze.

"Trent?" Tessa questioned.

"Put your seat belt on."

"Okay…"

Before any more time could pass, Trent cranked the engine and pulled down the street. He glanced in the rearview mirror just in time to see the men turn and stare.

They were on to them.

It would take Leo's men some time to get to their car, which meant that Trent had to move quickly and carefully.

The thugs would most likely assume Trent and Tessa would take the road out of town, in the opposite direction from which they'd come. That was why Trent decided to hang a left and head around the block. They'd go back in the direction they came, but take a different route, one away from Leo's henchmen.

"They're still following us," Tessa said, peering behind her.

Spontaneously, Trent turned left and swerved into a side street. He wasn't going to lose them as easily as he'd hoped. He had to make a split-second decision.

Seizing a window of opportunity, he pulled into an open garage bay at an auto shop. As soon as he threw the car into Park, he hopped out and lowered the garage door.

"What are you doing?" someone said behind him.

Trent ignored whoever was speaking for a moment and remained beside one of the windows, holding his breath as he waited.

"Sir?"

Trent raised a finger, begging for the man's silence. Two minutes later, the car chasing them squealed past, not even glancing in their direction.

His heart slowed for a moment. Maybe they'd lost them. He had to be patient, though, and make sure they'd really lost them. His hope was that the men would assume Trent and Tessa had headed toward the interstate instead of hiding here.

"Now, would you care to explain what's going on?" the voice behind him asked.

Trent turned and spotted a kid—he was probably in his late teens—staring at him, a wrench in his hand. An old Camaro was on a lift beside the boy.

Trent pointed to the garage door he'd lowered. "Sorry about that. It's just cold outside. I was wondering if you'd mind checking my oil?"

The kid still stared at him. "You don't know how to check oil?"

"I'm a little out of practice." Trent shrugged and did his best to look sheepish. Of course he knew how to check the oil. That excuse had been the first thing that came to his mind, though.

"Look, I get it. You're trying to hide something," the kid said.

Trent glanced out the window again. Still no sign of the men pursuing them. But they were on borrowed time. "What do you mean?"

The boy pointed back and forth between Trent and Tessa. "Are you two sneaking around, like in some kind of forbidden love story?"

The kid didn't seem like the *Romeo and Juliet* type. Obviously, he watched too much TV.

"No, no forbidden love," Trent said. "But if you must know, we are playing a little game of hide-and-seek. You caught us."

"Please don't rat us out," Tessa said, sticking her head out of her window.

The boy smiled. "As long as you're not here

when my boss gets back, I couldn't care less. It's kind of fun to see adults your age having fun."

Trent ignored his remark and continued watching out the window.

"Any sign of them?" the kid asked, obviously having no idea just how dangerous this game was.

If those men came back, Trent would have to get the teenager out of here and quick. "Not yet."

"I can open the door on the other side and you can sneak out that way. It leads to an alley that ends right on the edge of town."

Trent stared at the boy a moment, surprised at his willingness to help.

The teen shrugged. "I play a lot of video games where I pretend to be hiding from the law. I've thought this through a few times."

Trent glanced out the window again and saw no one. Maybe—just maybe—his plan had worked.

"Thank you," Trent said.

They climbed back into the car, snapped their seat belts in place and waited as the boy opened the other garage door. He rolled down his window and handed the kid a twenty-dollar bill.

"Good luck!" the boy called.

Trent pulled out slowly and scanned his surroundings. There was still no sign of the other car. He started the opposite way from which they'd come, on guard in case it appeared again.

"I'm glad the boy was the only one in the garage," Tessa said.

"Tell me about it."

"Do you think we lost them?" Tessa asked, still slunk low in her seat.

Trent glanced in the mirror again. "I hope so. But we're not out of the woods yet, so to speak. They'll canvass the area for us. We need to get somewhere we can disappear for a while."

"Leo has a lot of resources. He'll utilize whatever he needs."

Tessa looked so alone as she said the words. Betrayal could do that to a person—make them unwilling to ever trust again. He knew the feeling all too well.

"It sounds as if Leo really hurt you," Trent said, pulling out of town and remaining cautiously optimistic.

She snapped her head toward him. "What?"

"Leo. It sounds as if he really hurt you."

She pulled herself up in the seat and frowned. "We had one of those whirlwind romances. I thought he walked on water."

"So that made it even harder when his true self was revealed."

"Exactly." She crossed her arms. "I never in my wildest dreams thought that this would happen. I saw a wedding in my future, kids, the perfect house. I went from being in the art world and wearing business suits every day to this."

She waved her hand up and down, showcasing her worn jeans, flannel shirt and sloppy ponytail.

"I actually think that's a pretty nice look on you," Trent said. Then again, he'd always preferred women who looked comfortable in their own skin to women with bleached hair, overdone makeup and uncomfortable-looking clothes.

Even though Tessa's face turned a tinge of red, she continued as she if she didn't hear him. "The man I thought I loved is now trying to kill me. It's possibly the worst ending to any fairy-tale romance that I could ever conjure up in my mind."

"I can only imagine how hard that was on you." His and Laurel's story hadn't supposed to have ended the way it had, either. But sometimes life just didn't work out the way people planned, and all one could do was make the best of the circumstances given.

She nodded. "Eye-opening to say the least. Definitely made me realize that I'm better off alone than I am trusting other people."

"You mean, trusting the *wrong* people."

She shook her head. "No, people in general. These months on my own have been kind of nice. There's been no one to let me down."

"Come on, you can't tell me that being alone is

better than being with your loved ones. I hardly know you, but I can tell that much about you."

"I miss my family. I trust them. But I can't ever see myself having faith in others. Not after Leo."

"That's a shame. You'll be missing out. Life is much better when you share it with other people." He'd told himself that so many times. He felt like a hypocrite saying it now, because he certainly hadn't lived it out. He still held people at arm's length.

"And whom exactly do you share your life with?"

He swallowed hard. That was a good question. "I have friends."

"But you're probably married to your career, right?"

He swallowed hard again. She'd nailed him. No doubt, there was truth in her words. He had pulled away since Laurel died. He'd tried to keep his mind occupied with anything other than his pain.

Tessa didn't push anymore, and he didn't say anything. He continued driving, trying not to let her words bother him. At one time, his life had been full, as well. He'd had his friends in the police academy, and their comradery was unmistakable. Then he'd become a detective and been engaged to Laurel. Her family had lived close and they'd spent endless weekends having barbecues and cookouts and watching football games on TV.

All of that had changed when she'd died. Her family still blamed Trent, and he couldn't argue against their feelings. If Laurel hadn't been associated with him, she'd still be alive now.

He'd given up his career as a detective, started this PI practice and in the process become somewhat of a loner himself.

No, he didn't have any room to talk.

As they traveled farther down the road with no sign of the men behind them, Trent finally allowed his foot to ease off the pedal some. The day was gray with thick clouds above them, and the temperature was dropping by the minute.

He could really use some coffee, but no way was he stopping for any. "Did you buy any water?"

Tessa pulled a bottle from the bag, twisted the top and handed it to him. "I also have some crackers, muffins and a sandwich. Anything tempt you?"

"I'll take the sandwich. You should eat something, too."

She peeled back the plastic on the ham and cheese and handed it to him. Then she fished out some peanut-butter crackers for herself.

"How's my family doing?" she asked, her voice cracking.

"Your mom has been having some heart problems, if you want to know the truth."

Tessa rubbed her chest. "Really? My poor mom… I wanted to spare her all of this."

"Leo spun a pretty convincing tale about you," he said. "I didn't go into all of the details earlier, but he said he broke up with you after he caught you stealing money from the gallery."

"What?" Her eyes widened with shock.

Trent nodded, knowing the story was only going to become harder to swallow. "He said you needed the money because of all of your credit card debt."

"I don't have any debt. I only had one credit card in case of an emergency!" She shook her head and leaned back into the seat. "He had it all worked out, didn't he?"

"He was convincing when he told your family he'd do anything in his power to help find you."

"Of course he did! He wants to find me so he can kill me. They didn't believe him, did they?"

Trent shrugged. "The truth is, Leo brought in paperwork—evidence—to support everything he told them."

"He manipulated people or paid them off in order to get them on his side. He has people on his payroll who can create false backgrounds and financial histories. I can't believe this, yet at the same time it's not surprising."

"I know this is tough to hear, but you asked and I thought you should know everything."

Lord, please. Help.

Again, desperation was leading her back to exploring the possibility that God actually cared.

What if He doesn't answer your prayer? a quiet voice asked. *What if He doesn't answer it in the way you want? Will you still be open to the idea that God is a loving God?*

She tried to shut out the voice.

God doesn't work like a vending machine. You don't put twenty-five cents in and get the candy of your choice. Faith is about trusting Him whatever the outcome.

Where was this internal conversation coming from? Maybe all of those days of growing up in Sunday school were coming back to her. Answers that she'd thought were buried were coming to the surface.

Perhaps she'd stopped trusting God just like she'd stopped trusting people. Maybe that was her biggest mistake of all.

Before she could dwell on it any longer, the car lost traction. It slipped across the ice, gliding dangerously in the direction of the cliff. Each second seemed to pass in slow motion yet incredibly fast at the same time.

Tessa gasped and reached for the dash to steady herself.

The snow made it impossible to see how close they were to careening off the mountainside. But for the third or fourth time in twenty-four hours, her life began to pass before her eyes.

She wasn't ready to go yet. She had conversations to finish, family to see, a relationship with God she had to make right. Plus, she still needed to clear her name.

Her eyes flung toward Trent. Though his gaze was intense and his grip tight on the steering wheel, he remained in control. That thought brought Tessa immense comfort. If anyone could maneuver out of this tricky situation, it was Trent.

With dizzying, mind-perplexing movement, the car slowed, slid and flirted with deadly danger.

Finally, the vehicle stopped gliding and came to a slow halt.

Trent glanced over at her, visibly releasing his breath. "That was close."

"Too close."

He grimaced. "I think this is the end of the road for us. It's too dangerous to go any farther."

"So what are we going to do? Just sit in the car wait for the storm to pass?"

"That's not safe, either. There are too many unknown factors. Too much risk of another car coming this way and ramming us. That would send us off the edge of this cliff."

"What are you suggesting?" She thought she knew the answer, but she hoped wrong.

"We're going to have to go and find shelter. On foot."

ELEVEN

Trent didn't want to do it. He knew the risks involved in leaving the safe confines of the car. But he also knew the dangers of staying in one place. The snow was coming down so hard that he couldn't tell where the road started or ended. There was no way he could attempt to drive again, not after that tailspin they'd just experienced.

Tessa was tough. He'd seen the strength in her gaze. Sure, she might be scared, but fear made people's reactions sharper. It could work to her advantage right now.

Despite that knowledge, his heart sank with compassion when he saw the trepidation on her face. The task before them was huge and would overwhelm anyone. Go walking in a snowstorm on a mountain road? It wasn't ideal.

"If you say so," she finally said.

"I'll check and see if there's anything in the trunk. Meanwhile, zip up your coat and tuck the legs of your jeans into your boots. Also, take the food we have and see if you can store it in your jacket. We're going to need everything we can get."

She nodded and began preparing for their journey.

Trent opened the door and a gust of frigid air rushed into the vehicle, confirming what he already knew: this was going to be hard. Arduous. Grueling.

He put his foot down, expecting to feel the ground. Instead, he felt air.

He sucked in a breath as he realized what that meant.

"What?" Tessa asked.

"We were only about two inches from going over the mountain."

Her eyes widened. "Wow."

"I'm going to have to climb out of your side. Carefully."

She nodded stiffly. "We can do this, right?"

He reached out and squeezed her hand. "We can. We just have to stick together, okay?"

She nodded again. With one more deep breath, she opened her door. More cool air rushed inside, attacking any warmth left on their skin. Carefully, Tessa placed her foot on the ground, tested it to make sure the solid surface beneath her was real and then stepped out.

Wasting no more time, Trent climbed across

the seat and stepped out behind her. He watched each step carefully, uncertain where the ground began and ended. He opened the trunk and was relieved to see there were a few supplies that had been left by the previous owner, including a blanket and a flashlight. He took the blanket and wrapped it around Tessa's shoulders. Her coat was heavy, but she'd need all the warmth she could get.

There were also a couple of pairs of old work gloves. They'd be sufficient to protect their hands against the elements.

"Let's go." He put his hand around her arm so they could stick together.

As snow battered their faces, they started down the road. The weather had turned brutal and he wasn't sure what was colder: the snow or the wind. Trent prayed Tessa would be okay.

Every once in a while, the downfall would ease slightly and he could make out the wall of rock on one side of them. As the ground declined steeply down into a river gorge, he could see the treetops on the other side.

Trent hoped that once this section of road broke, maybe a house would appear. A driveway. Anything.

They couldn't stay out here in these conditions for too long. But if they'd remained in the car, they'd be sitting ducks, and those men could have come upon them. "You okay?" he asked Tessa.

She squinted against the snow but nodded.

Every few minutes, he glanced behind him. Usually, all he saw was white. But this time, something else caught his eye.

A light appeared.

Two lights.

Headlights.

Tessa followed Trent's gaze. "A car! We should flag them down. Maybe they can help."

Before she could say anything else, Trent pulled her against the rock wall beside them. He pressed himself into her. She wanted to complain, but the heat he brought with him made the words stick in her throat.

"What are you doing?" she whispered. She had the strange desire to bury her face in his chest. Just to keep warm, she told herself. Not because he was her knight in shining armor.

"We don't know who that is," he told her, his breath hot on her cheek.

Her heart thump-thumped out of control—from the adrenaline of the situation, not from Trent's closeness, she assured herself. How many times would she have to mutter that to herself before she was convinced?

"But—"

His gaze locked on hers. "We know Leo's men are out there looking for us. We can't take any chances."

His words sank in. He was right. But her cheeks were so cold. Her nose. Her fingers. Her feet.

The coolness had crept through her jeans, through her shoes. Soon it would probably sink through her coat. If she survived Leo's men, frostbite just might kill her.

"Will they see us?"

"Our coats are covered in snow. I think the chances are good that we'll blend in. Just don't make any sudden moves."

Only moving her eyes, she glanced in the direction she'd seen the headlights. They were upon them.

She held her breath, waiting to see how the situation would play out. She prayed they'd be invisible.

"What do you see?" Trent asked.

"They're getting closer."

At once, visions of the car sliding on ice and hitting them filled her mind. There were so many dangers in being out here right now. All she had to do was take her pick of various fear-inducing scenarios.

"They're slowing down," she whispered.

"Are you sure?"

She watched carefully. "I think they're stopping."

"If they see us, just follow my lead, okay?"

She nodded. That was fine, because she had no idea what else to do. Running through the snow didn't seem like an option. There were too many unknowns.

"They're backing up," she muttered.

"Really? Can you see anything else?"

"I think it's them, Trent. The car is brown. A sedan. I can't be sure, but…"

"Just keep a cool head. Let's see how this plays out."

She nodded, Trent's words helping to ground her. He was right. They couldn't let panic alert these men to their presence.

"They found the car," Trent muttered. He took her arm again. "We're going to start moving—slowly and carefully, until we can't see them anymore. If those men realize that was our car, they're going to come after us. We need to put some space between us and them."

"I agree."

He tugged her forward, still remaining close to the wall. Thankfully, the mountain curved away from the car behind them and helped them to disappear out of sight for a moment.

A sign appeared in front of them.

"Snow Current," Trent read. "One mile ahead."

"That's the ski lodge!" Tessa said.

"Ski lodge?"

She frowned. "But it's closed. From what I heard, it was booming about ten years ago until the economy forced the place to shut down. It's been abandoned ever since. My boss, Chris, as well as a few of my clients at the travel agency, used to talk about the place, but I've never been there."

"It's shelter. We need to make it there. It's only another mile. Can you do it?"

She nodded, eyes squinted and head lowered as gusts of cold, frosty air assaulted them.

"I can." Even if the thought caused dread to fill her. She wanted out of this snow. Now.

The rock beside them disappeared, and Tessa sucked in a breath, feeling the unknown swirling around her. Maybe it was the cold. Maybe it was messing with her mind. But she felt as if she'd just stepped out into a white abyss. The ground under her felt like packed ice but gave no indication if there was asphalt there still or if they'd veered off the road.

Trust. This was all a matter of trust, she reminded herself. She was going to have to learn her lesson and make some decisions…fast.

Though the snow concealed them, Trent couldn't help but feel exposed. They were walking into the great unknown, uncertain of each of their steps.

His gut told him that the men had discovered their car. If Leo's men had found the car, Trent had no doubt they would search ardently for them.

They'd been dressed in SWAT gear last time Trent had seen them. Then, at the café, they'd worn long sleeves with khakis. With any luck, those men weren't dressed to be in this weather. He only hoped that would work to his and Tessa's advantage.

Whatever happened, they had to get somewhere warm. These conditions could cause serious damage to their health. They needed a fire, to eat, to get warm.

He glanced behind him. Headlights.

The men were attempting to come after them in their car.

This wasn't good.

He grabbed Tessa's arm. "We've got to move."

Her eyes widened, but she didn't ask any questions. Just then, the rock wall beside them bent, allowing for some extra room. This was probably a roadside pull-off, Trent realized, remembering some of the small areas he'd seen that sported a small parking area, picnic tables and scenic overlooks. This might be the perfect place for them to hide. He pulled Tessa into the cove and instructed her to stay low. A picnic table was there, covered in snow. They crawled beneath it.

Trent kept an eye on the headlights.

The car stopped.

Slowly, the vehicle seemed to disappear.

They were slipping, Trent realized.

The car had hit a patch of ice and they couldn't make it up the mountain road anymore.

"What's going on?" Tessa asked.

"The road is too slick for them to continue, especially with this incline."

"That's good, right?"

"As long as they don't set out on foot."

"Trent?" Tessa whispered.

"Yes?"

"If we don't make it out of this alive, I just want to say thank you."

"Don't talk like that," he told her, his heart twisting with emotions he hadn't felt in a long time.

"No, I need to say this. You've gone above and beyond. Any sane person would have left me on my own by now, set me up to fend for myself. You had no obligation to stick with me, but you did."

Did she really think that he would have abandoned her? He wasn't that type of person. He'd set out to do a task and he intended on completing it. "We're going to be okay, Tessa," he assured her.

"Thank you, Trent."

He'd had no idea when he'd agreed to this assignment that this was what it would turn into. The danger had been much greater than he'd thought, as this case went much deeper than a simple missing person investigation.

Tessa's life was on the line. By default, so was his. Not only that, but his heart was getting involved. He could deny it all he wanted, but his feelings for Tessa were already starting to move beyond that gut-level attraction he felt toward her. He wasn't ready for that.

Even more worrisome was the realization that the safety of many people in this country was at risk.

Several minutes passed and finally Trent felt it was safe to leave. The men must have turned around and headed back. Their search would probably resume when the weather broke.

Trent and Tessa started their upward climb again, battling the elements, the slick road and their waning energy. Tessa's steps were becoming slower. Her breathing was heavier. Her face was red.

His heart panged with regret. He wished there was something he could do to help her. But their only choice was to keep moving.

One mile. On an ordinary day, that distance wasn't unthinkable. But in this weather—and in the mountains—it would take much longer. He estimated they were halfway there. Once they reached the abandoned ski lodge, it could still be a hike to get to the first building.

Lord, give us strength. Show us Your way. Protect Tessa.

They marched forward, one step at a time, no clue as to what was around them. The snow beat down, creating a white shield in every direction they looked. The elements battered them, made it hard to communicate, caused friction as their bodies collided with the air and snow.

Just as his foot hit something—something that felt more hollow than the ground prior—Tessa slipped out of his grasp and disappeared into the white below.

TWELVE

Tessa felt the ground vanish from beneath her. The air rushed from her lungs, and she let out a gasp. Before she realized what was happening, gravity pulled her downward in a free fall.

Her arms flailed.

Her feet kicked.

A scream stuck in her throat.

Finally, instinct kicked in. Her hands connected with something. She clawed at the slippery surface just within reach.

A brief window of opportunity.

A small chance to save herself.

Her body jerked to a stop. Her arms ached at the impact, her joints immediately sore from the harsh jolt.

But it didn't matter. She wasn't falling. Not for the moment, at least.

Her fingers had somehow managed to grip a wooden beam. Immediately, her arms burned under the strain of holding her weight. Her gloved fingers felt uncertain, weaker than she'd like, as if this was only a temporary fix.

Against her better judgment, she looked down. A swirling white mass beckoned beneath her.

The river, she realized.

This was a bridge.

She'd stepped off a bridge.

It suddenly all made sense, and her fear intensified.

This was going to be a horrible way to die.

As if to confirm that, her hands began to slip.

She couldn't hold on much longer. She wasn't strong enough. Her gloves were too slick. She was too cold.

Mom, I love you. I'm sorry you had to endure all of this. I wish I could have seen you again. Tell everyone how much I missed them.

If only her mom could hear her final words.

Lord, I'm sorry for how I must have let You down. I'm sorry I realized too late how important You are in my life. Please forgive me. I want to do better. I want to do right.

Her hand slipped again. Her heart raced as she felt her last inch of security disappearing.

Suddenly, Trent's hands covered hers. His face came into view. "I've got you, Tessa."

With an unnatural amount of ease, Trent gripped her hands and pulled her from where she dangled. She landed in the snow behind him.

Her heart raced.

She was on solid ground.

Finally.

Thankfully.

Trent knelt beside her, his eyes full of concern, his chest rapidly rising and falling with adrenaline. "Are you okay?"

She nodded. "I think so."

"Let's get you on your feet, then."

He helped her up. As soon as she put weight on her leg, she yelped in pain. When she looked down, she saw that her jeans were torn and blood gushed out.

"You must have cut yourself on the way down."

"I'll… I'll be fine." As soon as she said the words, she tried to take a step and nearly fell. Her face squeezed with pain.

Before she could contemplate her options, Trent swept her up in his arms and began walking. Apparently they were wasting too much time and had to move.

"I can't…ask you…to do this," Tessa said, her face still scrunched with discomfort.

"You didn't ask. I just did it."

Trent had been trained to travel in these conditions. He'd fought in Afghanistan—in both the dry and arid deserts and in the frigid mountains. Tessa hadn't.

Her strength was fading, and fast. He had to hurry.

At the moment, she seemed to melt in his arms. Her head flopped against his shoulder. Her lips were pressed into a tight line.

"We're going to be just fine, Tessa," he murmured.

"I can't ask you to do this," she whispered.

"Like I said, you didn't. I once carried one of my comrades in arms five miles up a mountain toward help," he told her, trying to keep her talking. "He weighed twice as much as you."

"What happened?"

"Roadside bomb. He got hit. I didn't. Our vehicle was destroyed. If we were going to get out of that village, we had to walk."

"I guess you escaped?"

"We did. My friend is doing just fine today, you'll be glad to know. Just like you'll look back one day and realize how crazy all of this was. It will be in the past tense. You'll move on." As he said the words, his heart lurched. Why did it bother him to think about her moving on one day? He had to put those thoughts out of his head.

"I hope so," she whispered.

He pushed forward, breathing easier once he knew he'd crossed the bridge. The lodge should just be a little farther up this road. Once there, maybe Tessa could get warm. He'd look for a first-aid kit. Maybe start a fire.

When Trent had seen her go off that bridge, his heart had dropped. He couldn't let Tessa die. He'd sacrifice himself if he had to. He'd feared he wouldn't be able to pull her from where she dangled.

But when he'd seen the absolute fear in her eyes, he knew he had to do everything within his power to do so. Leveraging himself while trying to reach her had been a struggle, but by God's grace he'd done it.

He continued to push forward, step by step. Slowly, the lodge got closer.

He glanced down at Tessa and saw her eyes had closed.

"Tessa," he called.

There was no response.

He shook her slightly. "Tessa."

She moaned.

This wasn't good. Trent had to get her somewhere warm, somewhere he could properly bandage her wound. They'd made it this far—he couldn't give up now.

Just ahead, during a break between snow gusts, another sign appeared—Snow Current. The insignia didn't have a "distance ahead" designation. No, it was a welcome sign.

They were here! They were at the lodge. Now he just needed to find a building to give them shelter.

He had no time to waste.

The snowstorm eased. He wasn't sure how long the interruption would last, but he was grateful for it. Maybe it would give him just enough time to find shelter.

Ahead, he saw a large lodge-like building. That was where they would go. It wasn't the closest building, but it was the one most likely to have a fireplace. Even though the smoke would be a giveaway that they were here, it was a chance he had to take.

Because he was determined to keep Tessa alive.

Tessa had wafted from lucid to delusional as she rested in Trent's arms. She'd drifted off for a moment and, in that instant, she'd been back at home with her family. They'd been laughing. She'd felt safe.

Even stranger, in her quasi dream Trent had been by her side.

The image had left her feeling warm and cozy. Too happy. What she needed was to keep her distance from Trent. It was the only way she could protect her heart—by remaining solo, and not getting attached.

It had been so long since she'd felt safe and loved that the dream had just seemed to mock her, to show her what she was missing.

At once, she pulled her eyes open. She sucked in a deep breath at the unfamiliar place surrounding her.

A fire crackled beside her, a blanket—blankets, for that matter—were piled on top of her. The room around her was large, almost overwhelmingly so. It smelled dusty and looked neglected.

Finally, Trent's face came into view. Everything came back to her. The men hunting them. The snowstorm. Falling from the bridge.

In each of those instances, Trent had saved her. She'd be dead now without him.

Her heart filled with gratitude. And maybe something else. The thought made her throat tighten with both joy and fear.

"How are you feeling?" he asked, peering down at her with concern in his eyes.

Had he been sitting there beside her the whole time? Watching her? Making sure she was okay?

Her cheeks flushed at the thought.

She tried to sit up, but her leg jolted with pain. That was right—she was injured. She'd almost died, for that matter. How had she gotten here? Trent must have carried her the entire way.

"You have a pretty deep cut," Trent said, tucking the blanket around her. "I cleaned it and put a bandage on it. Right now, we need to concentrate on getting you warm."

"How about you? Are you—"

He shook his head, his gaze steady and almost somber. "Don't worry about me. I'll be fine."

At his words, a shiver raced through her and a deep ache seemed to reach down to her bones, despite the warm fire crackling beside her. "It's so…cold."

"You'll warm up soon." He reached under the heap of blankets and found one of her hands. He began rubbing it in his own.

His touch—however utilitarian it was—caused her cheeks to warm. He was only trying to save her from frostbite, yet his touch was too tender for that. His hands, though callused, felt gentle.

Her gaze wandered the area as she tried to focus her thoughts on something other than Trent. They were in a huge room with a ceiling that stretched at least three stories high. Bright windows lined one wall, displaying the blizzard-like conditions outside. Huge wooden beams strapped the edges of the room, and the fireplace was probably taller than Tessa and surrounded completely in what looked like river rock.

"You found it," she whispered. "The ski lodge."

And somehow he'd managed to get her here,

start a fire and remain intact himself. Maybe he was a superhero.

His eyes followed her for a brief moment. "I did. I built a fire and found some blankets in a few of the old rooms. I haven't been able to explore much else."

"How long was I out?" As she said the words, she realized how dry her mouth was. It felt like sandpaper. Not to mention the fact that her lips were chapped and peeling.

She inwardly groaned at the thought.

She could only imagine what she must look like. Not that she cared. She wasn't trying to impress anyone. But she could have died out there. If Trent hadn't been quick in his thinking and reacting, she would have fallen to her death into the river below that bridge. Even more, if he hadn't gotten her here, she could have frozen. She knew she wasn't home free yet, but her odds were greatly improved, and not by anything she'd done herself.

"We've been here for about an hour." He continued to rub her hands.

"Any sign of Leo's men?" She didn't even want to ask; she hardly wanted to know. Couldn't she just deal with one emergency at a time? She wished she had that luxury.

Trent shook his head. "No, not yet."

She didn't miss the *yet*. But she pushed the

thought aside for now. They'd deal with that later. Hopefully much later.

She looked at Trent for a moment. It was the first time she'd been able to study him without suspicion. His cheeks were red and his hair glinted, probably from the snow.

That was when she caught a glimpse of it—the kindness in his eyes. It was the real deal, not something that was fake or meant to impress. Trent McCabe was a good, decent man.

"Don't worry about me." He let go of her hand, and she immediately missed his touch. He scooted back and stood. "I'm going to see if there's anything I can use to heat up some water. Some fluids would do us both good. You stay here and get warm, okay?"

She nodded, already missing his presence even though he hadn't left yet. "Okay."

As he retreated, she turned toward the fire. The glorious heat emanating from it warmed her face and thawed her frozen extremities. In the middle of all of this craziness, being here in the lodge at the moment felt like a little oasis. Sure, the blankets smelled musty. The whole place appeared abandoned, maybe even a little haunted. Snow blanketed the outside and the floor beneath her was cold.

But for just a moment, she felt she could

breathe. She'd take whatever comfort she could get and hang on to it for as long as she could.

At once, she imagined this place as it might have been at one time. She pictured visitors in ski suits standing around, sipping hot chocolate and talking about the slopes. She envisioned families together, friends chatting, strangers bonding over their love of adrenaline rushes.

Now it was desolate. Forgotten. Empty.

Don't let yourself become just like this ski lodge.

She blinked as the thought entered her mind. Where had that come from? Why were all of these esoteric ideas hitting her? It was almost as if a force greater than herself was calling her back.

As though God was speaking to her in a quiet, gentle voice.

"I found an old pot."

Trent's voice plucked her from her thoughts. She looked over and saw him walk into the room with a cast-iron skillet and two coffee mugs. "That's great."

"There's no water here, so I used some snow to wash it," Trent said. "Now we just need to warm this snow up and we'll be in business."

Against her will, she shivered again. The motion was immediately followed by her teeth chattering. The reaction was so sudden, so strong that it surprised her. "I guess I'm colder than I realize."

"That's a good thing," Trent said, already working at the fire. "Your body is reacting and trying to keep you warm. It's a survival mechanism."

She nodded but felt overcome by her reaction. It was as if every single thing in her life was out of control—her body, her emotions, her circumstances. *When everything was stripped away, you learned who you really were.* That was what her dad had always said.

She'd been on a crash course these past several months, then.

She actually liked some of the things she'd discovered about herself. She was capable. She could survive without a latte from the drive-through every morning. Fancy restaurants were overrated. Those were the surface items she'd realized.

On a deeper level, she'd found she enjoyed having some peace and quiet, that family was more important than any job and that sometimes less was more.

With a somewhat contented sigh, she watched as Trent put the pot over the fire and gently stoked the wood there.

The man really was tough. He had to be cold, but he had some kind of inner strength that pushed him to keep going. A silent sense of responsibly caused him to put her needs above her own.

That thought did something strange to her heart.

She was entering dangerous territory, she realized. And she needed to put a stop to it before she ended up getting hurt again. This man was just doing his job. That was it.

She couldn't allow her thoughts to go anywhere beyond that.

Trent kept an eye on Tessa, hoping she didn't take a turn for the worse. When they'd arrived here at the lodge, she'd been totally out, and he'd feared he wouldn't be able to wake her. Thankfully, he'd started the fire and some color was returning to her cheeks. Despite that, her hands were still cold.

The cut on her leg was deeper than he'd like. She really should get to a hospital, but since that wasn't an option right now, he'd cleaned the wound and wrapped it with some bandages he'd found in a cabinet in the old kitchen. The wrap was a little brittle with age, but it would work.

While she'd slept, he'd found an old radio and picked up a signal. To his dismay, a news report had caught his ear. The police were searching for a man and a woman in connection with an explosion in Gideon's Hollow, West Virginia. The woman was identified as twenty-seven-year-old Theresa Davidson who might be going by the alias Tessa Jones. Anyone who'd seen her was asked to report information to the police.

Had Tessa been set up again? First by Leo after she'd fled, and now by Leo as she ran for her life? That was certainly how it appeared. He must have gone to the authorities and revealed her real name.

As he glanced down at Tessa, his heart lurched in ways it shouldn't. Even being half-frozen, she was still lovely, especially with the firelight dancing across her face. Warmth had returned to her eyes, which was a good start. That meant that she was warming from the inside, also.

He poured some water from the pot into a mug. Though he wished he had some coffee to go with this, he didn't. At least the water would be warm. Carefully, he brought it to Tessa and helped her to sit up. He feared she couldn't remain upright on her own, so he let her lean back on his chest. She fit a little too snugly there.

"See if you can take a sip of this. It will help you warm up," he urged, bringing the cup closer.

She didn't argue. Tentatively, she put the cup to her lips and took a sip. "That was a crazy storm. It started, what? Three hours ago? It already looks as if a foot has fallen."

"It came on fast and heavy, that's for sure. If we hadn't found this place, I'm not sure we would have made it. The good news is that because the storm came so fast, Leo's men shouldn't be able to follow our footprints. They're also not dressed for this weather. But while we're safe here for a time, we can't get too comfortable."

"I wouldn't put anything past them." She paused with her water raised to her lips. "Please drink something yourself, Trent. You need to get warm, too."

He didn't want to admit it, but sitting here beside Tessa made some kind of internal warmth surge through him. But she was right. He'd be no good to her if he didn't take care of himself, also.

Reluctantly, he moved away from Tessa for long enough to pour himself some warm water. He wanted to move back beside her, but he'd lost the chance. She was sitting up fine on her own. Instead, he lowered himself in front of her, near the fire. The heat from the flames felt good and for the first time since they'd gotten here, he allowed himself to relax for a moment—if only ever so slightly.

They'd survived their last battle. Soon they'd have to prepare themselves for the next. Right now, he needed to recharge.

"I bet this place was a beauty at one time. Don't you think?" Tessa asked, her head falling back so she could see the ceiling.

"Definitely." The old building was fascinating. It looked almost as if the owners had left the place in a hurry—there were still pictures on the walls, a couple pots on the stove in the kitchen. Just what had happened here?

"Do you ski?" Tessa asked before taking another sip of her water.

He shrugged. "I've been a few times. I prefer being on the water to being on the snow."

She smiled softly. "Me, too. I only went skiing once, and it was with Leo's family. It was somewhere up in Pennsylvania, and there was no expense spared." Her smile slipped into a frown. "I didn't realize at that time that all of those luxuries were paid for with money exchanged for innocent human lives."

"You didn't know."

Her frown deepened. "I didn't even question it. I just assumed their wealth was from the art gallery."

"It was a natural assumption. Art can be a lucrative business."

"I just feel so naive about everything—about Leo, his family, his money, his friends. I never considered myself a pushover before, but my eyes were definitely opened to how much of an optimist I can be."

"There's nothing wrong with being an optimist. I'd take an optimistic any day to some who's jaded and skeptical about everything. The world needs people who aren't afraid to trust." He took a sip of his water, grateful for a hot drink.

She straightened. "Well, that's not me anymore. Now I'm suspicious of everyone. I fear I've gone to the opposite extreme."

He met her gaze. "You haven't. You only think you have."

A flush rushed over her cheeks and she looked away.

Something passed between them in that moment, and Trent knew he'd let the conversation get too personal. He needed to get his focus back here. There was a time for survival and a time for romance. Right now was a time for survival.

He scooted toward some items he'd laid out by the fire and picked up a sandwich. "Here you go. It's not frozen anymore."

She eyed the sandwich a moment before taking it.

He picked up the other half and began eating, also. The bread was soggier than he would have liked, but it was good. Nourishment could be the difference between surviving or not.

As he glanced out the window again at the falling snow, he realized staying alive involved more than a man-against-man struggle. They were also battling nature.

He prayed that the storm would only protect them, and not be their demise.

THIRTEEN

"Sit tight for one minute," Trent said after he finished his sandwich. "I need to make a quick phone call."

Tessa nodded, curiosity creeping into her gaze.

He wandered out of the main room, but remained close enough that he could keep an eye on her and the windows—not that he could see much with the wall of snow that cascaded from the sky. But he had to remain vigilant in keeping watch. Those men were resourceful, so he wouldn't put anything past them.

He took the prepaid phone from his pocket and glanced at the screen, fully expecting not to have a signal out here in the middle of nowhere. To his surprise, one bar registered.

He silently thanked God, as it had to be by His grace that he was even able to make this phone call.

He punched in Zach's number, thankful he had it memorized. A minute later, his friend answered.

"I tried to call you back a couple of hours ago, but your phone went straight to voice mail," Zach said.

"Yeah, my phone is…indisposed at the moment. I have a new one." Trent shoved his shoulder against the wall, his gaze continuously surveying the area around him.

"Sounds as if there's a story there, but save it for later. I looked into this Leo McAllister. I couldn't find anything on him."

"Nothing?" Surprise rippled through him. That couldn't be right.

"Nothing criminal," Zach said. "Now, his family is a different story. On paper, they're squeaky clean. But I started digging a little deeper. According to my contact at the CIA, they travel abroad quite a bit and have been seen socializing with associates of people on a terrorist watch list."

"Really?" Not that he'd doubted what Tessa told him, but it was good to get another perspective. Zach was objective and his opinion on this would be invaluable.

"It gets better. Apparently, the McAllister family has been under surveillance for quite some time now. There was some kind of anonymous tip to authorities a little less than a year ago. Law officials haven't been able to find any evidence against them, though."

"Interesting." That anonymous tip must have been from Tessa.

"Listen, Trent, I don't know what your involvement is with this family," Zach continued. "But my friend said that the people they're suspected to have ties with are no joke. Apparently, there are two people associated with the family who've been found murdered. Again, there's no evidence tying the McAllisters to the crimes. Both are still open homicide cases. But I don't believe in coincidences."

Tension returned to Trent's shoulders, even stronger than before. He'd known these men were dead serious and lethal, but Zach only confirmed it. If those men captured them, he and Tessa would both soon be dead.

"What can you tell me about the murders?"

"The first was a delivery driver. One of the McAllister galleries was on his route. Name was Frank Webber. The other man worked at a bank. There's no direct correlation to the family, only that he played a game of golf with Walter McAllister once. Walter is Leo McAllister's uncle."

"The news just gets worse all the time," Trent said, his gaze going to Tessa again. She faced the fire, unmoving except for occasionally sipping her drink. She was tough, but everything they knew was going to be tested before the end of this. "I may need more of your help, Zach."

"Of course. Anything."

Trent didn't know who else he could trust. He could call the local authorities, but he doubted they'd take them seriously. Plus, if Tessa's old boss was right, the rumor might be spreading around town that Tessa was one of the bad guys. He couldn't put her in that position. Since these guys had the ability to disguise themselves as the police, that also made him cautious.

He gave Zach a brief overview of the twelve hours since they'd last talked.

"Sounds as if you're in over your head," Zach said.

Trent glanced at the snow outside again. It continued to pile up, at least a foot deep. "Literally."

"Well, it just so happens I have two weeks between my old job and starting my new one. What do you want me to do?"

"I need you to find out what the police know about Tessa. She's been set up and now there's an APB out for her arrest. At this point, I'm not sure whom we can trust, not even local authorities. The more information I can be armed with, the better. The person behind this obviously has deep connections."

"I can do that."

"I need one more thing—for you to pick us up. The roads are slick. But we're trapped out here and, again, I don't want to call the police. The fewer people who know where we are, the better."

"Let me do a little research, make some phone calls. Then I'll check road conditions and head out there."

"Thanks, Zach. I appreciate it."

He hung up, grateful to know help was on the way. Trent only hoped they could stay safe until Zach arrived.

As soon as Tessa stood from her huddle of blankets on the floor, she regretted it. Pain shot up her leg. One glance at the bandages strapped around her calf caused her to squirm. A deep ache rushed through her muscles when she stepped on her foot.

"You shouldn't put too much weight on it," Trent said, reappearing and shoving a phone into his pocket.

The action caused her defenses to go back up. Who had Trent called? Was he hiding something? A niggle of distrust crept in. There was something he wasn't telling her.

She shoved away her doubts. Trent was on her side. There was no reason to doubt him.

Except that nearly everyone she'd trusted had let her down.

That thought caused a knot to lodge in her throat. Usually when people kept information from other people, it was because they were concealing something. What was Trent not telling her?

"I need to get moving." She raised her chin, knowing she couldn't depend on Trent fully. The idea was tempting but not logical.

Trent wrapped his hand around her arm, his expression firm. "You need to rest."

"But—"

"I'll keep an eye on things around here. You need rest. Save your strength for the battles ahead."

She wanted to argue, to be stubborn. But the truth was she couldn't stand much longer. Nor could she walk without help.

Begrudgingly, she sat down. She wouldn't admit it, but it felt good to get off her feet. What would feel even better were a long bath and some fresh clothes. Maybe a warm meal and some coffee. None of those things were possibilities right now, though. She had to be grateful for what she had—life, breath, a heartbeat and a chance at a brighter future.

She looked up, waiting for Trent to say something.

He didn't.

Not about the phone call, at least.

Instead, he said, "I'm going to look around here and see what I can find. We're going to need more supplies—in case we have to stay for a while and in case the men find us. We have to be prepared."

He was going to leave her alone. Her fear deepened. She knew she had to be a big girl; it was just that she felt so much more secure and protected when Trent was with her.

How could she question if he was trustworthy one minute and feel so safe with him the next? It didn't make sense, not even to her. She wished her emotions weren't such a tangled mess. She wished her past didn't dictate her reactions to people today. But that was the way life worked sometimes, whether she liked it or not. Keeping her distance from people had helped to keep her alive for the past several months. She wasn't sure if doing the same would keep her alive or kill her right now.

"Not to be a broken record, but you really should take it easy," Trent said, that edge of authority still staining his voice. It was as if he always knew exactly what he was doing and felt 100 percent confident in his choices. Must be nice.

Tessa grimaced as her leg ached again.

"Don't worry—I'm going to stay in this building, so I'll keep watch," he continued. "But if we're going to last here for very long, I'm going to need some more firewood—dry firewood—as well as some blankets and food."

She nodded.

There was no way Trent was in on this in some way…was there? Leo was conniving, brilliant and manipulative. He wouldn't have planted someone like Trent in her life, would he?

But that would be the perfect plan. Allow Tessa to trust Trent and believe he was on her side. Meanwhile, he would lead Tessa right into the den of lions—right to Leo.

She shook her head. No, that thought was crazy.

Yet it wouldn't leave her mind.

When Trent walked back into the main lodge area, he was surprised to see that Tessa had drifted to sleep. Good. She needed to rest.

He deposited the pieces of some old chairs he'd found onto the floor. He'd use this for firewood. With the flames blazing and strong, he went back and grabbed some cans of beef stew. They were about a year past the expiration date, but he'd check to see if they were still good because often canned goods lasted long past the date stamped on the lid.

He'd taken note of the entire lodge. Aside from the four doors located in this room, there were six other doors leading into the lodge. He blocked the rest of them with dressers. The furniture wouldn't hold back someone determined to get in, but at least it would slow them down or alert Trent that they were coming.

The two of them should be good here for a while. But as soon as the snow slowed, they should try to make a run for it. Staying in one place too long would be a bad idea. But he wasn't sure how fast Tessa could move with her leg injured as it was.

Something strange had passed through her gaze earlier—was it doubt? In him? He was going to mention his phone call to Zach, but he feared she'd ask too many questions. She was under enough stress without learning that the local police were also looking for her. He hoped Tessa trusted him enough to follow his lead.

Laurel had always told him that he expected people to have confidence in him easily. Maybe it was because of his training as a ranger—they'd had no choice but to trust each other.

It didn't matter if Tessa believed in him or not. His one goal right now was to keep her safe. Not to earn her friendship. Not to make her like him. Not to soothe her with platitudes.

Only to keep her alive.

Despite his determination, something twisted in his gut at the thought. He knew why. It was because there was a part of him that really liked Tessa, that wanted to get to know her better, that wanted to wipe away the worry from her gaze.

Just then, she opened her eyes and he realized he'd been staring at her.

Staring at the lovely lines on her soft face. At her hair as it ruffled across the blanket behind her and at her lips as they gently parted.

He hadn't felt this fascinated with someone since…well, since Laurel.

"I can't believe I fell asleep." She pulled a hair behind her ear self-consciously. "Again."

"Your body is telling you that you need rest."

He went to the fire again and added some pieces of broken furniture. Once the flames grew larger, he opened a can of stewed beef. He dumped it into a pot and placed it over the fire.

"Who'd you call earlier?" Tessa asked.

He startled a moment. "Just a friend."

"Which friend?"

She wasn't backing down. "A friend in law enforcement. I'm getting him to help us out."

Her eyes held a look of discernment. She was trying to measure whether he was telling the truth.

"You asked me to trust you, yet you obviously don't trust me. Why were you keeping that quiet?"

"I didn't want to share anything until I learned more."

"And? What did you learn?"

He let out a breath, stoked the fire once more

and then settled back on the floor. "I learned that there are two suspicious deaths associated with the McAllister family."

"Who?"

"A delivery driver and someone who worked at a bank."

Tessa gasped. "Was his name Frank?"

Trent nodded. "I believe so. You know him?"

She squeezed the skin between her eyes, shoulders slumping. "Frank always made our deliveries. Every day. We talked quite a bit, and he was a lovely person. In his fifties, expecting his first grandchild, looking forward to taking a cruise. Of course, that was a year ago. When…?"

"About eight months ago."

"Around the time I left…" she muttered.

"Tessa, this probably didn't have anything to do with you. It was the master plan of a crazy killer."

"Maybe I should have warned him. Warned more people. Maybe I should have done more instead of running."

"Before you beat yourself up, I also heard that there was an anonymous call reported with information about the family."

She straightened. "Did the FBI actually research the tip I gave them?"

"Unfortunately, they couldn't find any solid

evidence so the McAllisters have just been under surveillance."

Her shoulders slumped again. "I managed to copy all of the files off the gallery servers and then erase their contact information before I fled. But in my haste, I dropped the thumb drive where I'd saved the evidence."

"Don't beat yourself up. The authorities are still looking for proof so they can put these guys behind bars. But for now no one's talking and the paper trail has disappeared."

"That's not surprising. The McAllisters have power and resources. They're good at covering their tracks. I didn't expect the cops to believe me anyway, not when Leo and his family are so active in the nonprofit community."

"Money and power definitely have reach. You'd be a fool to deny that. A lot of people can paint themselves as sheep when they're wolves."

"Biblical reference?" she questioned.

"Yes, definitely. It's refreshing to talk to someone who recognizes that."

"I might recognize it. I don't necessarily believe it, though."

"Why's that?" He stirred the stew, the savory scent of beef, potatoes and gravy rising up to meet him. He couldn't neglect food and sleep too long or he'd be useless.

"Up until a few days ago, I hadn't felt His presence in my life in a long time."

"You mean because bad things have happened?"

She shrugged. "You make it sound so simple. But maybe you're right. Maybe that's what my reasoning boils down to."

"Bad things happen because we live in a fallen world that's full of sin. The bad things are people's doing, not God's. But He can use them in our lives."

"I don't know. It certainly doesn't feel that way."

"Our relationship with Jesus was never supposed to be about feeling. That's a part of it. But emotions and feelings change. It's the same with every relationship in our lives. If we just depend on how we're feeling at the time, it will never last."

"You sound pretty smart."

"I've learned that lesson the hard way over the years. Believe me."

Something flashed through her gaze. Was it hope? Understanding?

Before he could identify it, he heard a crash.

FOURTEEN

Tessa jerked upright at the sound. *What was that?*

Trent was instantly on his feet, his stance showing the soldier he used to be, and the expression in his eyes so intense that she'd hate to be on the other side of the battle against him right now.

"Stay here," he ordered.

His tone left no room for argument.

She pulled the blankets more closely around her as she waited. What could that have been? It almost sounded as if a bomb had exploded. Had Leo's men found them?

Her gaze swung around. What if those men were out there now, watching her, ready to pounce?

She waited, each minute feeling like an hour.

Finally, movement caught her eye at the far end of the room. Her heart skipped a beat.

Trent. It was just Trent.

He strode toward her, a grim expression on his

face. "Part of the roof collapsed in the east wing of the building."

Her heart slowed—until she realized how serious that could be, also. "What does that mean for us?"

He stirred the beef again. "Nothing. We have no choice but to stay here. The collapse happened in what looks like the oldest part of the structure. I guess it couldn't withstand the weight of the snow."

She glanced above her at the thick wooden beams arching across a vaulted ceiling. "I hope this part is stronger."

"We'll keep an eye on it." He spooned some food into her mug and then handed it to her. "Here, eat this."

She didn't argue. The first bite was hot and nearly tasteless, but she was so hungry that she didn't care.

As she glanced out the window, she saw the sun was beginning to set.

"We should both try to get some shut-eye."

"I've already rested some. How about if I keep watch for a while?"

He nodded, grabbed a blanket and settled on the couch across from her. "That sounds good. If you hear or see anything that's at all suspicious, wake me. Promise?"

She nodded. "I promise."

As soon as Trent drifted to sleep, she forced herself to stand. Her face scrunched in pain as she put weight on her leg. But she had to do this. She had to walk a bit, see for herself what was going on here at the lodge.

Each step caused an ache to pulsate through her, but she made herself keep going, keep moving. Finally, she reached the window. She already missed the warmth of the fireplace and her blankets. But she couldn't allow herself to become too comfortable.

She stared outside. The snow was already to the window. Tessa estimated about sixteen inches had fallen today. The roads would be impassable, which was both a comfort and worry. It meant Leo's men might not be able to reach them, but it also meant they might not be able to leave if they needed to.

Her conversation with Trent drifted back to her. He made sense. Maybe her faith in God should be more than something that changed based on her emotions.

The one thing she appreciated about Trent was that he didn't make promises based on emotions. He didn't manipulate. What she saw was what she got. She admired that, especially after being around Leo.

Just then, Trent muttered something. Tessa

stepped closer and saw that he was still asleep. He was obviously having some kind of dream.

His shoulder jerked, as if he was fighting some kind of unseen force. He grunted again.

Tessa looked away, feeling as though she was being intrusive.

Just as she stepped back toward the window, Trent said something discernible.

"Laurel."

He'd said the name Laurel.

Who was Laurel, exactly? Was Trent's heart already taken?

How could Tessa have been so foolish? Of *course* someone like Trent would be taken. Here she'd been letting her feelings grow for a man who was unavailable. She should have known better.

More than ever she needed to stick to her plan: accept his help but keep her distance. Her emotions had been heightened; in the process, they'd grown out of control.

Experience should have taught her the danger of letting her emotions roam free. It was never a good idea. In fact, in the past it had only led to heartache.

Suddenly, she stepped back from the window as a chill washed over her.

She didn't know what had caused it. Her imagination? Caution over everything that had happened? Or was there real danger out there, getting closer and closer?

She wasn't sure.

But she decided to go back to the couch where she'd watch and wait…and try not to think about the handsome man who'd stuck by her through thick and thin.

Trent took the second shift, noticing as they switched roles that Tessa seemed a bit more distant than she had earlier. Maybe it was the lack of sleep. Maybe the stress of the situation was getting to her. He didn't know.

As she lay on the couch, he couldn't help but marvel at how peaceful she looked in the middle of all of this craziness.

Laurel had always looked so peaceful and hopeful. She'd been a kindergarten teacher, something she'd dreamed about since she was in elementary school herself. His heart still sank when he thought about how her life had been cut short.

He wouldn't let that happen to Tessa. He'd sacrifice his life if he had to in order to protect her.

He peered out one of the massive windows lining the lodge again. Only darkness stared back. Were the men out there? Were they watching?

His gut told him no. Not yet, at least. It was only a matter of time before they found them. As soon as it was daylight, Trent needed to check out the rest of the property and see if there were any resources here that could help them.

At least the snow had stopped. Forecasters had been correct. There was more than a foot piled up outside.

He glanced at his phone and briefly thought about calling Tessa's family to give them an update. But telling them that he'd found their daughter while he and Tessa were on the brink of so much danger didn't seem wise. Still, he knew her loved ones were waiting, still hoping, that Tessa would be okay. They'd lived with so many doubts and uncertainties for so long.

He'd wait, he decided. He wanted to hear back from Zach. He wanted to get somewhere safe and have a few more reassurances. Then he'd make the call.

"Hey," a groggy voice said.

He looked over and saw that Tessa was awake. His heart skipped a beat at her tousled hair and sleepy eyes. Even in this state, she was a vision, one of those natural beauties who needed little help to look good.

He glanced at his watch and saw that she'd gotten a few hours of shut-eye. It was better than nothing. "Morning."

"I feel as if I've been hit by a truck."

"Days like yesterday can do that to you."

"Has it really only been less than two days since all of this started? It feels like weeks."

"Hard to believe, isn't it?" He strode over to her and handed her some the last package of crackers. "Here you go. Eat up."

She didn't argue. Instead, she shivered, pulled the covers closer around her and then ripped the package open. "Anything new?"

He shook his head. "Sun should be coming up soon. I'll fix some hot water for us so we can stay hydrated. Then I'm going to head out."

"Head out?"

He nodded. "I need to see what else is out there. We won't get very far on foot, Tessa."

"So you're suggesting we cross-country ski instead?"

Her light tone made him smile. When he nodded at her leg, his smile faded. "Not with your injury."

"I'll be fine."

"Well, see if you say that after you put some weight on it."

She took a bite of her cracker then swallowed. "Can I ask you something?"

"Sure." Her tone indicated this was serious.

"How is my mom paying you? You've been working this case for a while. If you charge an hourly rate, I can only imagine how high the cost of your investigation is. I know my mom doesn't have that much money."

He didn't say anything for a moment.

"Please tell me Leo isn't helping?"

"Leo put up money as a reward."

She frowned. "Go figure. But that doesn't explain your fees."

"I'm waiving them."

Her eyes widened. "Really? But why?"

"Because I've grown rather fond of your family. I couldn't give up on them. I couldn't squeeze them dry for this case."

"That's…that's kind of you."

He shrugged. "Your mom has me over to eat about once a week. I've been invited to church with them, to birthday parties. They're starting to feel like my family."

A sentimental smile feathered across her lips. "That sounds like my family. But how are you managing to pay your bills?"

"I still receive some money from the army. Plus, I take on odd jobs here and there. Things that aren't really that interesting but that pay the bills. I have some savings."

"That's really kind of you, Trent. Thank you."

"Don't thank me yet. Not until we get out of this situation." He stood. "Speaking of which, I think I see some daylight peeking over that mountain. I'm going to go see what I can find."

"Be careful," she said softly.

"I will."

The snow was deep and cold outside. Trent sank in it up to his knees, which made the walk treacherous. He had little choice, though. In the first building he came to, he found a snowmobile. With some tinkering, he discovered it was still operational. He also found an old can of gas and filled it up. This could definitely come in handy later.

Throughout the rest of the building searches, he found a few more cans of food, some changes of clothes and more things he could use as firewood.

In the back of his mind, he thought about both the men after them and the caved-in ceiling. By all appearances, Tessa was safe right now. The structure seemed sound. But he had to stay watchful.

Remaining in one of the old cabins, he checked his phone. No messages from Zach.

He rounded the back of the lodge on his way back. He wanted to make sure the building looked out.

What he saw froze him in his tracks.

There were footprints. Leading right to the back window and…to one of the doors.

Tessa mindlessly straightened blankets and stoked the fire and paced—in the name of physical therapy. At least that was what she told herself.

Really, she was anxiously waiting for Trent's return. What had he found? Anything? The results of his outing could mean the difference between hope or despair.

She was praying for hope.

As she paced to the window, she squirmed at the pain in her leg. The good news was that it wasn't broken. The bad was that the cut was deep and it would slow her down. Talk about bad timing.

As she stared outside, she thought about Trent spending time with her family. The realization was so bittersweet. She could easily see him fitting in.

And his kindness in taking on this case for little to no pay warmed her heart.

Then she remembered Laurel. It was best if she didn't let her heart go crazy and start daydreaming about what it would be like to hold Trent's hand or pretend he might care about her away from this crazy situation they were in. It had just been so long since she'd felt a connection with anyone. She realized she missed being part of a community, a tribe, a team.

Maybe there were people out there worth trusting.

Suddenly, she paused as a foreign sound teased her hearing. It had almost sounded like a footstep. Had Trent come back?

She swirled away from the window and scanned the room around her. It looked the same as always. Nothing suspicious.

If Trent had returned, he should be here any minute. He always used the same door down the hallway to keep the cold air in the room at bay.

She waited a few minutes, but he didn't appear.

Apprehension crept up her spine. If not Trent, then what was the sound?

The caved-in roof, she remembered.

Maybe that was what it was. Was more of the ceiling about to collapse on them? Or maybe the part that had already been destroyed was crumbling more?

No, she told herself. She could have been hearing things. After all, everything seemed silent right now.

Why couldn't Trent be back? She hated to admit it, but she felt much better when he was close by. Again, those crazy emotions of hers were leading her astray, causing her to toss back and forth between trust and distrust, dependence and independence.

She scanned the area behind her, which was the hallway leading to the old kitchen, according to what Trent had told her. Again, nothing looked out of place. What was going on?

Just as she reached for her gun, she heard the footstep again. She turned around just in time to hear something click beside her. A man stood there.

An evil grin spread across his face. "You didn't think you'd get away from us that easily, did you?"

At the sound of his heartless voice, her blood went cold.

FIFTEEN

Just as he feared—someone was inside with Tessa. Trent ducked behind the corner. How had the man found them? It wasn't important. All that mattered was figuring out how to get out of this situation. He'd worry about the other details once Tessa was safe.

Moving quietly, he crept inside, making sure to stay concealed and out of sight. From where he stood, he had a perfect view of everything that was happening. A man—he recognized him as one of the men who'd confronted them at Chris's house—stood in front of Tessa. He had two things that frightened any warmth right out of Trent: a gun and a diabolical smile.

"I radioed my other men," the man said, flaunting his Smith & Wesson in front of Tessa.

The man wanted to invoke fear; he enjoyed scaring other people. He was the kind of person Trent despised. It took everything in him to remain calm.

"They should be here any moment," the man continued. "The snow slowed us up. But all of this was just a matter of time. We never lose our guy—or girl. That's not going to change now."

"What do you want from me?" Tessa stared at the man, not fear in her eyes as much as anger. Her hands were braced on the couch behind her and she favored her uninjured leg. But she wasn't shrinking. Trent could admire that.

"I'm just doing a job. Leo wants to handle you himself."

She leveled her gaze at the man. "I take it you're okay with a man beating up on a woman."

The man grinned, not even a speck of goodness or mercy in his eyes. "I'm okay with getting paid for a job I was hired to do. Well paid, at that."

"I hope there's enough money for you to live with yourself when this is all said and done."

His smile slipped some. "Enough talking. We just need to wait here until the rest of my guys arrive. Where's the man you came here with?"

"There was…an accident as we walked here. He didn't make it."

The man stared at Tessa a moment, as if trying to read her. "You don't seem too broken up about it."

She shrugged nonchalantly. "What can I say? We weren't close. He was hired to find me, just like you were. However, he was ten times the man you are. He'd never hurt a woman."

Her words warmed Trent, but only for a moment.

"Too bad he's not here now. He might have been able to help you out." He reached for her, his gun still drawn. "Now, I need to figure out what to do with you to bide my time. I can think of a few ideas."

Tessa gasped as the man squeezed her arm and pulled her toward him.

Fire coursed through Trent's blood. He drew his gun from his waistband and aimed. In one clean shot, Trent hit the man's shoulder. The man cried out in pain and dropped his gun. Tessa scrambled to retrieve the weapon, and she raised it toward her attacker, also.

Trent's heart slowed. But he knew the battle wasn't anywhere near being won.

Tessa gasped for air as Trent grabbed her arm and pulled her away from the man. They'd tied him to a chair, knowing his friends would arrive soon enough to help him. In the meantime, he'd be indisposed.

Trent reached down and grabbed something from the ground. "Put this on."

She held up the puffy white snowsuit. "Where'd you find this?"

"One of the cabins. It's going to be cold where we're going."

She didn't ask any questions. At least it sounded

as though he had a plan. That was more than she could say for herself. He pulled another coat on over his own and then pulled on a hat. He handed another to Tessa.

"When they find you, they're going to kill you," the man in the chair grumbled. His gaze looked haggard and every once in a while he moaned with pain. But he was still angry and determined.

"I'd worry about yourself right now," Trent said.

The man let out a deep growl before his face squeezed with pain.

"Now, come on," Trent said, turning his attention back to Tessa. "We've got to get out of here before the others arrive. We don't have much time."

She lifted a two-way radio that had been clipped to her attacker's belt and listened for a brief moment. "It sounds as if the rest of the guys are within eyesight of the lodge."

He nodded, as if impressed that she'd thought ahead enough to grab the device. "Good to know. This way we can stay a step ahead of them."

He grabbed her hand and pulled her outside. The cold air was brittle and frosty. It took Tessa's breath away for a moment. But she had no time to dwell on it. Trent pulled her forward and she let him. A few flakes from the treetops scattered

"Thank you."

Trent stared ahead at the windshield. "Is that snow?"

It had been gray and especially cold all morning. But snow? He'd hoped it would hold off.

Tessa nodded. "They were saying a snowstorm was headed this way."

"What did they predict?"

"A foot of snow in a five-hour time range. That was the last I heard."

His gut churned. That wasn't a good outlook. They were not in a car suitable for any kind of snowstorm or bad weather.

"It's only the beginning of November."

She nodded. "I know. The brutal weather is getting an early start this year."

They needed to make it as far away as possible before the storm arrived. Because there was no way they'd make it otherwise.

Tessa's stomach still didn't feel full, but at least she had some food to settle it. As she watched the snowflakes come down harder and faster, a ripple of anxiety shuddered through her. Driving these roads in the snow was hazardous, even for the most experienced driver. Trent had purposely stayed on back roads. By all appearances, they'd lost the men who'd been after them, but Tessa had a feeling this wasn't over yet. Leo would indeed do everything he could to find them.

Trent had a white-knuckled grip on the steering wheel. The roads were getting slippery, Tessa realized. And the steep drop-offs on one side of the stretch of asphalt made this all the more treacherous.

"Any idea where we are?" Trent asked.

She shrugged. "I think we're north of Gideon's Hollow."

"Any small towns up this way? I'd even take a big one."

"We're in mountain country. I didn't take much time to explore during my stay here, but you can go miles out here without running into much except cliffs, rivers and inclines."

He didn't say anything.

She studied his stoic expression a moment. "This isn't good, is it?"

He shook his head, his gaze remaining focused out the front windshield. "If the snow comes down any harder, I won't be able to see. It's practically a whiteout."

"Should we pull over?"

"We'll see."

The sinking feeling in her gut sank even lower. Why did this situation keep getting worse? As if it wasn't bad enough that Leo's men were after her. Now it had to snow.

downward and chilled her cheeks and eyelashes even more.

The wind slapped her cheeks as they rushed through the snow. Of course, rushing through the snow was like rushing through quicksand. Each step tried to suction them to the ground. They trudged forward regardless.

Another building came into sight. Tessa hoped that was where they were headed, because her legs were becoming numb again. At least that meant she couldn't feel the throbbing ache from her wound.

"In here," Trent urged. He pulled her into the building.

Just as they stepped inside, the radio at her waist cackled to life. "I see the building, Windwalker. What's the situation inside?"

Trent took the radio from her. "Targets are constrained. Waiting for help escorting them."

"Roger that. Should be there in less than five."

Trent and Tessa exchanged a look. They had to hurry.

"Come on," Trent urged. He climbed onto a... snowmobile?

"Where did this come from?" Tessa asked, climbing on behind him with a touch of trepidation.

"It must have been left here when the resort closed down. I found some gas and finally got it hot-wired so it works again. All I know is that I'm not complaining. Hold on tight."

Her throat constricted at her nearness to Trent. "I am."

He took her hands and pulled them tauter around his waist. "Don't be shy."

Her cheeks heated but only for a minute. She didn't have time to dwell on the solid muscle beneath her hands or the broad back her cheek was pressed against. She had to focus on survival.

The radio crackled again. "Where are you, Windwalker? We're inside the building." A curse followed. They must have found their guy tied up.

Wasting no more time, Trent burst through the door of the garage. The vehicle hit the snow and sprinkled flakes around them. Any other time it would be amazing. Right now, it seemed like a blur.

Just as they sped down the slope, three men stepped from the building, guns in hand. Keeping one arm around Trent, Tessa reached into her waistband and pulled out the Glock. Using her best aim—which was difficult because of the speed and the movement—she took a shot. Even if it didn't hit them, maybe it would scare them off some and buy them a little more time.

Finally, they cleared the lodge. The men were no match for their speed on the snowmobile.

"Where are we going?" Tessa asked as reality set in.

"I have no idea."

"To the main road?"

"Too dangerous. They'll look for us there." He headed toward the woods instead.

"And this is going to be better? You know there are cliffs around the gorge here, right?"

"Now I do."

She sucked in a breath and closed her eyes. No, she couldn't afford to close her eyes. She stole a glance behind her instead. The men were still chasing them, coming on foot. It was good they weren't on the road—they'd likely be located much easier. But still, the thought of journeying into the white wilderness ahead of them was unnerving.

Trent swerved as a tree appeared in their path. The landscape became thicker and harder to manage. They had to slow down. And that meant that the guys chasing them had a better chance of catching up.

Just then, a bullet whizzed by, lodging itself in a nearby tree. Splinters of wood flew at them.

Tessa looked behind her. Their pursuers were no longer running. It was worse.

"They've got sniper rifles out!" she yelled.

As he turned again, a trail came into view.

Perfect. At least this would make their journey easier and less treacherous.

Just as the thought entered her mind, another bullet whizzed by, narrowly missing them. She held on tighter to Trent as the trail became steeper.

The snowmobile slipped, but only for a moment. They whizzed away until the bullets could no longer reach them.

Thank You, Jesus.

Her relief was short-lived, as a fence appeared. If they didn't slow down, they'd ram right into it the tall stone structure.

Trent swerved, trying to miss the wall in front of them. The snowmobile teetered, and he feared it might tip. Snow sprayed behind them at their sudden movement, and Trent's heart raced as he anticipated what would happen next.

They came mere inches from hitting the wall, from tipping over. Thankfully, the vehicle righted. He let out a breath of relief.

He didn't ease up on the accelerator but kept going. They didn't have any time to waste. But this wall, this fence, was going to be a problem. He wasn't sure if it stretched all the way around the resort or not. But somehow, they had to get off this property. Otherwise Leo's men would definitely find them, and Trent couldn't let that happen.

He followed the wall, hoping to find a gate.

There had to be a service entrance around here somewhere that led to the main road.

The snowmobile hit a stump buried under a drift and the vehicle slowed. This was going to be tough. The terrain was too thick to be navigated easily by a snowmobile, but he was going to push the vehicle as hard as he could. He only hoped that the men chasing them didn't think ahead and search for a service entrance, also. If so, Trent and Tessa were on borrowed time.

Bingo! Just as he suspected, there was a gate up ahead. Now he prayed that it was unlocked or at least old and rusty so he could break through.

He slid to a stop and jumped off, instantly rattling the chain connecting the two wooden doors of the gate. It was old and rusty, yet still solid.

This wasn't good.

"Here, let me try," Tessa said.

She pulled out a cheap-looking multitool kit, similar to a Swiss Army knife, and began fiddling with the latch. He watched carefully, curious as to what she was doing and where she'd gotten the knife. Obviously, she was attempting to pick the lock. But why in the world did she think she could?

To Trent's surprise, the lock popped open. She jerked the chain down and pushed the gates open triumphantly.

"How...?" Trent started.

She shrugged as if it wasn't a big deal. "In addition to my self-defense and gun classes, I also learned how to pick locks. It seemed useful."

"The toolkit?"

"I found it in the glove compartment of the car. I slid it into my pocket before we abandoned the vehicle, just in case it came in handy. Looks as if it did."

"How fortuitous." Wasting no more time, Trent and Tessa climbed back onto the snowmobile and took off down the service road, grateful for the smoother surface. They'd make better time this way.

The cold air slapped him in the face and nearly took his breath away. But he couldn't think about it now. All that mattered was getting away as fast as possible.

As he traveled he put together snippets of a plan in his mind. Hopefully he still had phone service, because he needed to call Zach and see if his friend could pick them up ASAP. Then they needed to enlist more help. Find evidence. Put an end to all this.

He kept his eyes open for a break in the trees. If he found one it could mean the highway was approaching. He hoped this back road had cut enough time off their travel that Leo's men wouldn't be able to catch up for a while.

As Tessa's arms tightened around him, he wondered if he was projecting his past onto her. Was that the reason he felt so determined to see this through? He knew he had an innate sense of justice. He wouldn't leave a woman stranded without help. But it wasn't just his nature. He knew that how he felt about Tessa ran deeper than that. Though they'd only known each other a couple of days, the stress of this situation had quickly deepened their bond.

A clearing appeared in the distance. That had to be the road leading from the ski resort. It was going to be slick from the snow, but he hoped it was still passable. The road crews probably hadn't made it this way yet, since the only thing up here was the abandoned resort.

He slowed, but only for a moment, as he reached the narrow stretch. He spotted no one approaching from either side, so he carefully maneuvered the snowmobile onto the asphalt there. Once he was steady on the street, he started away from the ski lodge.

This was a different road, he realized. They would have passed their abandoned car by now otherwise. Here, a river snaked far below, probably breathtaking in other circumstances. If he could only make it far enough that there was some sort of landmark where Zach could find them.

"Trent, they're behind us," Tessa said.

He glanced back and saw a car headed their

way. The men were still far away, but that meant they only had a little time. Plus, they were running out of gas. He guessed they had five minutes max.

"Do you trust me?"

She hesitated before saying, "Yes."

"Then, we're going to have to jump. Okay?"

"Jump? Are you crazy?"

"It's our only choice. As soon as there's a good spot, we've got to get off and hide."

"Okay." Her voice was stained with uncertainty.

He couldn't blame her. The possibility was daunting.

He saw just the place up ahead. It was a grove of trees they could duck behind. It would be perfect. But he had to time it just right.

As the area approached, he slowed slightly. On a mental count of three, he eased off the accelerator, swung his leg over the snowmobile and grabbed Tessa. They jumped into the embankment beside them.

He prayed the risk paid off.

SIXTEEN

Trent and Tessa rolled across the ground, tumbling over each other several times before coming to a stop. Snow cocooned them, burying them with cold, icy layers.

Tessa found herself nestled on top of Trent. Her eyes widened at their closeness. Or perhaps it was the snow, the exhilaration of what they'd done or the astonishment that they'd survived. Whatever it was, her heart beat out of control.

She had to get focused.

Laurel, she remembered. She had no right to be attracted to or having feelings for this man.

"Don't move!" Trent whispered, obviously unaffected.

She remained still, all too aware of his presence. Wanting to slide off. To run.

But instead she stayed still, willing herself to break their gaze. Instead, her eyes went to his lips.

Bad idea.

All she could think about was how they might feel against hers. Which she had no right to do. It didn't matter that she'd misread the bond between them. She had to put an end to this.

Instead, she stared at the snow, hoping Trent couldn't feel her heart thumping out of control against his chest.

Just then, she heard a crash.

The snowmobile had gone over the ledge.

Tessa prayed Trent's plan worked and that the men assumed Tessa and Trent had gone over the cliff, as well. If not, they were both goners.

The sound of a vehicle crunching through the snow shattered the silence around them. Leo's men. This was the moment of truth.

Would they be discovered?

"You're doing great," Trent whispered, his voice light in her ear and his breath soft and warm on her cheek.

She forced herself to keep her eyes focused on the snow. She feared Trent might see a glimpse of her attraction to him. And that was all it was—a moment of attraction. After Leo, she knew she was better off alone.

The vehicle slowed and finally there was a moment of silence. It had stopped, Tessa realized. Only feet from them.

Had they been spotted?

A car doors opened. Feet clomped on the packed snow on the road.

"The snow must have gotten the best of them," one of the men said. "It looks as if their snowmobile went down the embankment and into the river below. The tracks lead straight off the road. The river is still flowing, though. It must have carried everyone away."

Silence—except for some footsteps. Were the men lurking closer? Would they be discovered?

Trent pulled his arms tightly around her, as if he sensed her anxiety.

The cold was starting to get to her again, too. Though Trent was probably shielding her from the bulk of the frozen snow below, there was definitely a coat of white iciness around her. It was beginning to seep through her hair, to tickle her neck.

They couldn't stay like this much longer.

"I'll send a crew farther downstream to look for their bodies," the man continued. "It was a big risk taking a vehicle like that out on this ice. Especially on roads like this."

Silence.

"You mean Grath? We found him, and one of our guys is taking him back to Virginia. We'll let your doctor look at him. People will ask too many questions otherwise."

Virginia. That was where Leo was still basing his operations. Wilmington Heights, maybe? Tessa stored away that information in case it came in handy later.

"All right. We'll clear the area and meet you. It looks as if this assignment is over. I know it's not the way you wanted it to end. But we got the same result."

Snow crunched again.

Tessa dared not breathe as she felt a shadow fall over her. The men were close—too close.

She continued to hold her breath, waiting to see what would happen next.

Finally, the shadow disappeared. Footsteps retreated. Car doors slammed.

A few minutes later, tires dug into snow and ice. The humming motor disappeared from earshot.

They were safe. At least for now, they were safe.

Trent gently prodded Tessa up, and they emerged from their snowy grave. Tessa glanced around. The men were gone. Thank goodness they were gone.

"I can't believe they didn't see us," Tessa said.

"Maybe that's because we have someone watching out for us."

She caught his gaze, surprised at the sincerity in his voice. "You mean God?"

He nodded. "Absolutely. I've seen Him answer prayers before."

She wiped the snow from her pants and jacket, unsure what to say except, "What now?"

"I'm calling my friend. I'm hoping he can pick us up—and soon." Trent gaze scanned the area around them. "In the meantime, we can't stand here. It's too dangerous, especially if those men come back to look at the crash site."

"Where do we go?"

He nodded up the hill. "There are some boulders up there. We should be able to take shelter behind there until we know for sure the coast is clear."

He took her hand and helped her up the incline, being mindful of her injured leg. Once they were settled behind the rock, he pulled his gloves off. His fingers were red, but he didn't seem to care. He pulled out his cell phone and dialed.

Tessa hardly heard him talk. The dampness was starting to trickle down her neck and into her clothing. She hoped—dare she say, prayed—that they wouldn't be out here too long.

When Trent hung up, he looked at her. "My friend is about twenty minutes away from the old ski lodge. He should be able to find us here. It's going to be okay, Tessa."

Something about the certainty in her voice brought her comfort. "What friend is that?"

"His name is Zach. We went to police academy together and worked on the force in Richmond for a while. He was a detective in Baltimore up until recently. He's one of the few people I actually trust."

He slipped his gloves back on and peered around the boulder.

"Do you see anything?" Tessa asked.

"Not yet. But we can't get too comfortable. How many men does this Leo guy have?"

"He can afford however many he wants. Money isn't an issue."

"It seems as though he has a whole army."

"For the right price, men will do anything." As she said the words, despair bit at her. Leo had even betrayed her for the right price, hadn't he?

He squeezed her arm. "Not all men."

The look in Trent's eyes made her throat go dry. Maybe all men weren't like Leo. Trent had proved himself to be honorable. It was just that she had such a hard time believing in people. She'd been stabbed in the back, and the pain of that scar made her afraid to ever put her faith in someone again.

She dragged her gaze away. "That's good to know."

Trent saw a green SUV pull to the side of the road and the headlights flickered three times. It was Zach.

He was just in time. If he and Tessa were out

here too much longer, there would be serious repercussions. The cold was biting, but it was the wind that nearly did them in. It blew down the mountainside, all the way through his jacket and layers of clothing.

"Come on." He led Tessa down the mountain, keeping one hand on her arm so she wouldn't lose her balance. Without wasting any time, they climbed into the back of the SUV. Heat filled the car, a welcome feeling after everything they'd been through.

"You two look terrible," Zach said.

"Good to see you, too," Trent said.

Zach flashed him a quick smile before turning serious. "I need to get you somewhere dry or, as my grandmother would say, you'll catch your death. I'm Zach, by the way," he told Tessa.

"Tessa," she said with a nod. Her teeth chattered together and her arms were drawn over her chest.

"Seat belts on. These roads are slick. Let's get out of here. I have the perfect place reserved."

Trent paused, waiting to see if Tessa needed help. It took some tugging, but she finally latched the belt in place. He pulled the strap across his chest also and settled back, happy to have Zach with them.

Zach tossed something in the backseat. "I thought you might be hungry. There are some sandwiches in there. I also have some coffee up here. Probably not hot anymore, but at least warm."

Trent took a cup and handed it to Tessa. She slowly took a sip and closed her eyes with delight.

"This is just what I needed," she said. "Thank you."

Trent took his own cup. The drink was tepid, but it was just warm enough to lift his spirits for a moment.

"Any updates since we spoke last?" Zach asked, glancing in his rearview mirror.

Trent glanced at Tessa before launching into a brief update. When he finished, his friend shook his head. "It sounds as if you're lucky to be alive. Both of you. And these guys who are after you, they're no joke."

"You don't have to tell us that," Trent said.

He had the strangest desire to pull Tessa toward him. To keep her warm. Purely for survival, he told himself. But he knew there was more to it than that. There was something about her that drew him to her, that made him want to be close.

When she'd been so near him in the snow after they'd abandoned the snowmobile, he'd thought he'd seen a flicker of attraction in her eyes, also. He hadn't allowed himself to even think about another woman since Laurel. But maybe something was changing inside him.

As they ate their sandwiches, Tessa was surprisingly quiet. All of this was a lot to process. "What now?"

Trent sighed and shook his head. She asked that question a lot, and he wished he had a good answer to give her. "I'm not sure if we'll outrun Leo. So we need to think of a way to nail him."

"If we have internet, I'm pretty handy with a computer," Tessa said. "I can probably hack into their system and see if they have anything new on file. I won't be able to get to their hidden files, probably."

"You think you can pull some information from their site?" Trent asked. "Maybe enough info that we could go to the FBI?"

She nodded slowly. "I'm sure they have more firewalls in place now, especially after what happened last night. My biggest worry is that the minute I hack into their server, they'll be able to trace where the hack is coming from. I can try to redirect it, but I can't guarantee how long that will last."

"We can't risk that." He shook his head. "We can't keep running. There's got to be another way."

"Maybe after this, there won't be any more running. I mean, I can probably scramble it for a certain time period. It might be worth the risk."

He shook his head. "You're in no position to run anymore. You need to see a doctor."

She didn't argue. Instead, she lay her head against the window and closed her eyes.

Good. She needed rest.

So did Trent, but he would never admit it.

"I don't need to tell you how serious this is," Zach said.

"By no means," Trent said, leaning forward. "I've been chased and pursued more ways than I can count. This nearly makes those terrorists over in the Middle East look like amateurs."

"I'd say you're going above and beyond the call of duty when it comes to being a private eye."

He shrugged and glanced at Tessa again as her chest rose and fell evenly with slumber. "I can't leave her alone in this."

"No, you can't. I'm glad I can help. My contact with the CIA called me back, Trent. One of those murders that was loosely associated with the family? It was a banker who'd apparently made some dirty deals. It wasn't a nice murder. Not that murder ever is. But the scene…it was brutal."

Trent cringed. Not that the news surprised him. But the confirmation did shake him up. He didn't want that kind of suffering to happen to Tessa.

"Where's this place we're going?"

"One of my old friends from Smuggler's Cove is ex-CIA. He works for an organization called

Iron Incorporated—they also go by Eyes—now. You heard of them?"

"The military contractors?"

"That's the one. He hooked me up with an old safe house operated by the agency. We should be out of harm's way there for a couple of days at least."

"Right now those men think we're dead," Trent said. "But they're looking for our bodies. When they discover we're not in that river, they'll resume their search for us."

"Maybe we'll have some answers by then."

"Maybe," Trent muttered. "We can only hope."

SEVENTEEN

When Tessa opened her eyes, a beautiful old Victorian house stood in front of her. She had to blink a couple of times to make sure she wasn't seeing things. Sure enough, it was like a real-life dollhouse. It was beautiful.

The place had turrets on both sides, siding that reminded her of gingerbread, multiple porches and even a corner gazebo with a swing. An inviting wreath swathed the blue front door and electric candles dotted the windows.

"Where are we?" Tessa asked, a touch of awe in her voice.

"It's where we're staying for the next couple of days," Trent said beside her.

Zach nodded. "Let's get you two inside. I'm sure a shower and some clean clothes sound good."

"Clean clothes?" Tessa questioned.

"I picked a few things up. Hope they're your size."

"I'm sure they will be fine."

As she climbed out she noticed the ache in her leg had returned. She'd probably have to have her wound looked at, as much as she didn't want to do that. She hoped she could hold off until this mess was done.

As always, Trent's hand went to her elbow. Did he think she wasn't steady on her feet? Was he just being a gentleman? She wasn't sure. She only knew that every time he touched her, waves of electricity coursed through her body.

They climbed the steps, Zach unlocked the door and they all slipped inside.

Before Tessa could even let her eyes explore her new surroundings, Zach directed her to a bathroom upstairs. "This one is all yours, Tessa. Trent, there's one downstairs you can use. I'll fix some dinner while you two get cleaned up."

Tessa didn't argue. As soon as the men retreated, she locked the bathroom door and took the warmest, most wonderful shower ever. It had never felt so good to wash all the grime away.

When she climbed out, she pulled back the bandage that Trent had wrapped around her leg. Blood had soaked through the gauze there and she knew she had to change it. She'd always been squeamish around blood.

As the deep gash on her leg came into view, her head spun. The cut was probably six inches long. And it was deep. Trent had put butterfly bandages across it, trying to seal it shut. She didn't see any signs of infection.

She found a bandage in the cabinet and then wrapped it up again. If this was the only scar she walked away with from this whole ordeal, she'd count herself fortunate.

She pulled on yoga pants, a long-sleeved turquoise T-shirt and fluffy socks with dogs on them. She dried her hair, wishing she had some makeup to cover up the circles under her eyes. But she had no room to complain, and she was thankful for what she'd been given.

She studied her reflection for a minute. This whole ordeal had taken a bigger toll on her than she'd expected. Her skin looked pale; her eyes had lost their glimmer.

Was she really going to let Leo do this to her? He could ruin a lot of the physical things in her life. But she'd let him ruin her inside, as well. She'd become a shell of the person she'd once been. That was giving someone a lot of power in her life.

Finally, Tessa stepped out of the steamy bathroom, not sure what to expect once she got downstairs.

Zach seemed nice enough and, if Trent trusted him, then certainly she could, too. He was tall, although not as tall as Trent, and he had blond hair with a slight curl to it. Inside the house, she'd caught a glimpse of blue eyes and dimpled cheeks.

What had Trent said? He was a detective somewhere?

She found the men downstairs, sitting at the breakfast bar and drinking coffee. They both got quiet when she walked in. Instead of feeling awkward, she slid onto the bench beside Trent. "Got any more of that java?"

"Coming right up," Zach said. He grabbed a mug and filled it for her.

Meanwhile, the scent of beef—steak, maybe?—sizzling on the stovetop made her stomach grumble. She was hungrier than she'd thought.

"About five more minutes until dinner is served," Zach said.

Tessa stole a glance at Trent. The man had always been striking. But right now, with his hair still glistening and the faint scent of soap emanating from him, her throat caught. He wore a long-sleeved black T-shirt that showed off his defined torso and a pair of dark-washed jeans. And despite everything they'd been through, he still looked alert.

By the time Zach set their food in front of them, Tessa was beyond hungry. She took the first bite of steak and it melted in her mouth.

"Where are you located out of now, Zach?

Baltimore?" She tried to remember what Trent had mentioned.

Something flashed through his gaze so briefly that Tessa thought she'd imagined it. "I was there for a while. I've found that I actually like being the sheriff in a small town, though. It makes the people you're serving seem more real when you see them every day and know most of them by name."

She nodded, not pressing it. "I see. Well, thank you for all of your help today. I don't know what we would have done without you."

"I hear you're pretty resourceful," Zach said.

Tessa glanced at Trent. "What did you say?"

"You can shoot a gun like nobody's business and pick a lock. I might recruit you as one of my deputies soon."

She smiled, despite the grim situation. "I don't like being a victim. What can I say?"

"Being proactive is good." Zach suddenly stood. "Look, I don't want to cut this short, but it's getting late. Just leave the plates in the sink, and I'll get them later. I'm going to check all the windows and doors one more time and then turn in for the night."

"Thanks again," Tessa said.

He tilted his head, almost as if he had a hat on. "No problem. Night, you all."

As soon as he disappeared, Tessa felt of a

touch of tension fill her. It wasn't that she was uncomfortable with Trent; she'd been around him enough to know that wasn't it. It was… She knew what it was. It was the fact that she was attracted to him. He made her feel jittery and unsure of herself and—

"So how are you doing really, Tessa?" Trent asked, turning toward her as they sat at the breakfast bar. A candle flickered between them and the lingering scent of coffee hung in the air. "You hanging in?"

She shrugged and leaned back, the wooden chair hard against her back. "I guess. What else can I do?"

"You want to go sit by the fire?" He nodded toward the other room where the warmth of the hearth beckoned.

"That sounds wonderful."

They walked into the living room. Tessa sat at one end of the couch and Trent draped a blanket over her before settling at the other end.

"Do you really think we're safe here?" Tessa asked. She didn't want to bring up the situation with Leo. She really didn't. She'd much rather pretend she was enjoying an evening with a handsome man. But that wasn't reality. Reality was that there were men trying to kill her and Trent's heart might already be taken.

"For a short time."

When he laid a hand on her leg, she drew in a deep breath.

"What? Your leg?" he asked.

She nodded, wishing she wasn't squinting with pain.

"Let me see it."

He peeled the blanket back and gently tugged up the leg of her yoga pants. "You bandaged it? You mind if I take a look?"

"Knock yourself out."

He gently unwrapped the gauze there and frowned. "I'd like to put some more medication on that, just to make sure it doesn't get infected."

Before she could insist she was okay and that he shouldn't fuss over her, he stood, disappeared and returned a few minutes with a first-aid kit. "A real one this time," he said with a small grin. Carefully, he took a towel and put it under her leg. "This is going to sting a little."

He poured some hydrogen peroxide over the wound. The liquid bubbled up, and she gritted her teeth at the sting.

"I know it's old-school to use this, but I've always thought it worked the best. Believe me—I've cleaned a lot of wounds in my day."

"As a ranger?" she asked, curious to know a bit more of his history.

"That's right."

"Why'd you get out?"

"It was time. I'd seen too much, felt too jaded, wanted to settle down." He patted the area around her wound dry and pulled out a tube of antibiotic ointment.

"So you became a police officer? Then a detective?"

He nodded again. "That's right. I did that for about eight years. Then I decided to go into business for myself."

"Why's that?"

His face went taut, and he began concentrating even more on dabbing her wound with ointment. "Long story. But I needed a change. Believe it or not, I'm usually a committed kind of guy. But sometimes you just can't ignore when changes need to take place in your life."

"I see." He didn't offer any more information, but, boy, did she want to know. What had happened to cause the sadness that crossed over his features? He wasn't willing to share, so she couldn't prod anymore, despite her curiosity.

Finally, he bandaged her wound, removed the towel and lowered her leg back onto the couch. He dropped the blanket over it and then settled back for a minute.

She felt she owed him something more than the bits and pieces of her life she'd shared. All he knew was that she'd dated a man who'd turned out to be a homicidal maniac. But there was so much more to the story.

She stared into the fire a moment, gathering her thoughts.

"There was a time I thought Leo walked on water," she started.

Her revelation seemed to startle him and he glanced her way, but said nothing.

"I was one of those girls who was really picky when it came to dating. I'd been out with guys before, but nothing really serious. I wanted to save everything for my one true love. Maybe I'd watched too many romantic movies. I don't know. But I didn't want to give my heart to someone if we weren't meant to be together forever." The memories came back stronger. "Then I met Leo. He swept me off my feet. I was working as the director at one of his art galleries. He was charismatic and handsome. He asked me out five times before I said yes."

"Five times? He didn't give up?"

"Leo isn't the type to give up." She cleared her throat. Leo had made that abundantly clear over the past few days, hadn't he? "Anyway, I finally said yes. I figured he'd try to impress me by taking me to a fancy restaurant and flaunting all of his successes. Instead, he took me on a picnic at a local park. We ate on a blanket, and he'd even made some sloppy sandwiches himself. I saw a different side of him that day. Maybe he wasn't the spoiled rich kid I thought he was. We were inseparable after that."

"It does sound like a whirlwind romance," Trent said.

"I literally thought he was the best thing that ever happened to me—until that day I caught him doing the arms deal. Then my eyes were truly opened to who he was. He'd been wooing me this whole time and keeping me distracted from everything happening right under my nose at the gallery. If I hadn't been so lovesick, I would have noticed that things weren't right. But I thought he could do no wrong."

"Love can be like that."

"In the blink of an eye, my life changed. I went from feeling like the happiest girl in the world to running for my life. Feeling betrayed. Feeling angry at myself for being so blind."

"It's not every day that someone's boyfriend is actually a terrorist in disguise. No one can really blame you."

"I blame me."

"Maybe you need to change that."

She stared at Trent moment. "You're right. I do. I was just thinking earlier that I'd let Leo have too much control in my life. That's a choice I made. I need to undo it."

Trent's admiration for Tessa grew. At first he'd thought she was a scared rabbit hiding in a little hole away from the rest of the world. But as the layers began to peel back, he'd realized that not only was she a survivor, but she was also protective of her loved ones.

She'd been hurt, but she'd also been prepared to face the consequences. Not many people he knew would take the initiative to learn how to use a gun, to pick a lock, to defend themselves.

As he stared at her now, the firelight dancing across her face, something squeezed in his heart. He wanted nothing more than to scoot closer, to touch her cheeks, to smooth away her hair.

He'd tried to extinguish his attraction to Tessa, but nothing he told himself seemed to work. No matter how he looked at it, Tessa was one of the most beautiful and intriguing women he'd ever met.

He saw the same look in her eyes—his feelings were mutual. Their emotions had grown quickly—a crazy situation like this could accelerate feelings. He had no doubt about that. But it almost felt as if there was something deeper between them that just a surge of attraction.

The fire dimmed, so he stood and stoked the

flames a moment. When he sat down again, he was closer. Her legs draped over his lap.

"This seems surreal, doesn't it?" she said softly. "Being here. Everything that's happened. I just want to let you know that if we don't get out of here, I appreciate all you've done."

He glanced at her and saw a tear trickle down her cheek. "Don't say that. We'll survive this."

"I know what these men are capable of."

Before he could second-guess his decision, Trent scooted closer and pulled Tessa against his chest. She didn't resist; instead she rested there. They sat in silence, neither needing to say a word.

EIGHTEEN

"Where's Trent?" Tessa asked Zach the next morning.

"He went outside to get some more firewood," Zach said. "He's one of those hardworking guys. Always dependable."

"I've noticed that," Tessa said, sitting at the breakfast bar. She glanced outside and saw Trent gathering wood in the snow. Her heart warmed at the sight.

How had her feelings grown so quickly? She not only felt indebted toward the man, but she also felt an unmistakable bond.

"Look, he's still reeling from what happened with Laurel. I don't want to see him get hurt again," Zach said, lowering his voice.

"Laurel?" Her pulse spiked.

He paused, squinting with thought—and maybe some surprise. "He hasn't told you about her?"

Tessa shook her head.

"He will when he's ready. In the meantime, I just want him to be careful."

Tessa got the warning loud and clear. Zach was protective of his friend. Tessa had no intentions of hurting Trent. She wondered what his story was and, once and for all, who was Laurel?

She'd trusted him with her own story, and she had to admit that it didn't feel good to know that Trent hadn't offered that same trust in her.

Just then, the back door opened and a gust of frigid air swept inside. Trent spotted Tessa and a smile tugged at his lips. "Good morning."

"Morning." Her return smile felt a little shy.

"I wanted to wait until you were both down here before I broke the bad news," Zach started, leaning against the kitchen counter, a new heaviness seeming to press on him.

Tessa instantly tensed in preparation for whatever he had to say. "Okay."

Trent sat beside her, and she found comfort in his mere presence.

"The bad news is that there's an APB out on Tessa," Zach said. "It's extended beyond Gideon's Hollow, beyond West Virginia and made it all the way to national law enforcement agencies. Someone reported that she was involved in a terrorism ring. Apparently, bomb-making materials were planted in the basement of the house she was staying in in West Virginia. She's a suspect in the explosion that took place at your cabin, Trent."

She gasped. "What?"

Zach nodded. "It's true. That makes a difficult situation even more difficult right now."

"That means the two of you could get in trouble, also. For being with me." Tessa's heart thudded with grief at the thought.

"You're being set up," Trent said, pulling off his gloves.

The grim lines on his face told the true story of what he was thinking, though: she had little chance of getting out of this situation. Either Leo killed her or she ended up in jail.

"Leo knows how to do it right," Tessa said. "What can I say? If they catch me, I'm dead. If the police find me, I'm locked up for life."

"I hate to continue with the bad news, but your face is on the news right now, also," Zach continued. "It says you've been going by an alias."

She squeezed the skin between her eyes as despair tried to bite deep. Maybe she should just turn herself in. That might save a lot of people heartache, including Trent and Zach.

"Leo knows how to play a sick game," Tessa said. "He's managed to trap me, no matter which direction I try to run."

Trent squeezed her shoulder. "We'll get through this."

She shook her head. "You should just let me go out on my own right now. I've already caused you both enough grief and upheaval. This was never either one of your problems to begin with."

"We can't let you do that," Trent said. "We're in this together."

"But you have a choice. You can get out."

"I choose not to," Trent said, no room for argument in his voice.

"Same here," Zach said. "You need all the support you can get. You'll never survive this alone. Men like these… They'll just keep coming after you until you're destroyed."

"Besides, I have an idea," Trent said.

Tessa turned toward him, her full attention on him. "Okay."

"You said when you downloaded all the information, you dropped the jump drive, right?"

She nodded. "Yes. After I copied it, I deleted it from their server so they wouldn't have access to their contacts. Unfortunately, the information I hoped to take to the police also disappeared in my moment of klutziness."

"Where did you drop it?"

"One of the vents in the office building." Her eyes widened as she realized what he was getting at. "You want to see if it's still there?"

He nodded. "I do."

"And how do you propose to do that?"

"I'd like to dress like an HVAC guy and say I came to look at their system."

"That sounds risky."

"It's going to take some planning, but I think it's feasible. However, I will need some help."

"You know my hands are kind of tied here, Trent. After Baltimore, I can't exactly run around like a free agent anymore," Zach said.

Trent raised his hand. "I would never ask you to do that. No, I need you to stay here and keep an eye on Tessa." He shook his head as Tessa started to object. "I know that's not what you want to hear, but it wouldn't be wise to leave you alone. You know what these men are capable of."

She couldn't argue with that. "You can't do it alone, though, Trent. Maybe I can help—"

"That's out of the question. One glance at you and we'll be made."

She couldn't argue with that, either. "Then, who? Who will help?"

"I know some guys," Zach said.

Trent and Tessa turned toward him, waiting to hear what he had to say.

"You know Eyes, that private security firm I told you about? They do freelance work. My friend works for them now. He might be able to assist."

"Let's see what we can put together, then. Tessa, you remember anything about the HVAC company they used?"

"At the gallery they used Thomas and Sons. They had for years. It used to be that Tom or one of his boys would come out personally. Of course, now that it's grown in size, I'm sure they have various employees that they send out. I can't guarantee the gallery still uses them, but it's a good guess."

"Zach, why don't you get on the phone with your friends and see if they can offer any assistance. Explain that this is a matter of national security. I'll research this company and see about putting together a van, a uniform—basically a cover story."

"Absolutely."

Tessa tried to remember the details of the gallery. Trent would need that information if he sneaked inside. He'd need the names of contacts if he wanted to appear legit.

She could hack into their server and find out that information for sure.

But there were risks involved. She had to weigh everything before making a decision.

But the possibility that she could do more to help continued to linger in her mind.

Trent put the finishing touches on his plans for tomorrow and stood. Normally something like this would take at least a week to put together. But they were on the clock and needed to move fast. God must have been watching out for them, because they had been able to get everything they needed in place at lightning speed.

Tessa had been a huge help today. It was more than her knowledge; he actually found himself finding comfort in her presence. They worked surprisingly well as a team. It was when they were on opposite sides of the field that things got complicated.

He made some coffee, grabbed two mugs and carried them both into the living room, where Tessa sat. He extended one to her. "Thought you might need a drink to warm up."

Her bright smile in return was all the thanks he needed. "Sounds like just what I need."

He sat down beside her—probably closer than he should have. He watched as she wrapped her hands around the mug, practically hugging it, and then she stared into the fire.

"I feel a little as though this is the calm before the storm," she said, glancing at him.

He let out a slow breath. "Maybe it is. But maybe after the storm has passed, this will be the norm and not the exception."

A light smile feathered across her face. "That would be nice. You seem so peaceful, even in the midst of all of this."

Suddenly, the weight on his shoulder seemed to press down harder. "I haven't always been like this. You asked me about why I became a PI?"

She nodded, a silent encouragement for him to continue.

"About three years ago, I put some pretty bad guys behind bars. They were gang members and responsible for the deaths of uncountable people. Mostly rival gang members, but there were a few who were simply innocent civilians who'd been caught in the cross fire. It was a really proud day for me."

"I can see why."

His shoulders became even heavier. "Unfortunately, my name wasn't kept hidden. It made the news. There were a few gang members that didn't go to jail—we didn't have any reason to hold them. I mean, you can't go to jail for being in a gang, only if you do illegal things while a part of it. Those men came after Laurel."

"Who's Laurel?"

"My fiancée."

All of Tessa's attention was suddenly focused on him. "Oh."

Even she seemed to sense that this story wasn't going anywhere pleasant. "I thought she was safe, but they found her. Before I could get to her, they put a bullet through her head."

"I'm so sorry."

He couldn't stop now or he'd never tell her the whole story. "I became obsessed with finding out who exactly had killed her. Made some bad decisions. Eventually they put me on desk duty. I reached one of the lowest points of my life. That's when my friend introduced me to Jesus, and I really found peace and purpose through that. I decided to become a PI so I could take on the cases that mattered the most to me."

"That makes sense. I know this probably doesn't mean much, but I'm so sorry, Trent." She put her hand on his biceps, her eyes an endless pool of compassion, kindness…and something more?

In a moment of decision, he leaned toward her. She didn't pull away. Slowly, certainly, he pressed his lips to hers. Emotions he hadn't felt in a long time hit him at full force.

"I hope you know not every guy is like Leo," he whispered.

Her eyes fluttered open, and a steady look of joy and trust filled them. "I know."

With that proclamation, he leaned toward her again, stealing another kiss. This one was longer, deeper and less tentative. He was enjoying being with Tessa a little too much.

He pulled away and stood. "We should probably say good-night. We need our rest for tomorrow."

"Good idea." He only prayed the hopeful feeling in his chest remained long after tomorrow was over.

* * *

Tessa couldn't deny the mix of exhilaration and fear that coursed through her. She didn't know where these feelings for Trent had come from or how they'd come on so fast. She felt a much deeper connection with him than she'd ever felt with…well, anyone. Even Leo.

And when she'd heard Trent talk about his fiancée, suddenly he made sense. His protectiveness made sense. His determination. His drive.

She didn't dare to tell him what she'd done earlier while he'd met with Zach. She'd sneaked upstairs and onto the internet. She'd hacked into Leo's server just long enough to confirm the name of the HVAC company, the lay of the building and the name of the new assistant at the gallery. She couldn't send Trent in without being certain.

She'd managed to scramble the servers, and it would be at least twenty-four hours before Leo's tech guys could trace where she was located. By that time, they'd have the information and could go to the FBI. She knew Trent wouldn't approve. But she'd done it for him. She'd own up to it once he got back.

She'd also looked for information that she could use against Leo, but his firewalls were too strong. He must have made them stronger after everything had happened with her. There was no way she could pull any new evidence from the reinforced system.

She'd thought about hacking into the system many times over the past eight months. But she knew she couldn't do that while she was living in West Virginia. It would have led Leo right to her. Plus, she'd had no one on her side. But now with Trent and Zach backing her up, maybe she had a fighting chance.

Trent…

Now, somehow, their lives were intertwined. But what happened when all of this was over? Would their lives ever return to normal? And what exactly was normal for Tessa? Would she actually be able to go home, to see her family? Could she look for a new job and start her life again?

The idea of all of this being over almost seemed too good to be true. There were so many things that could go wrong.

But for a moment—and just a moment—she dreamed about what it would be like to actually put this behind her. To actually trust again. To believe in someone. To put her faith in God.

She closed her eyes. *Lord, I want that peace that Trent has. I want to trust. I want to be a rock that doesn't move in the middle of a storm, instead of being tossed by every hardship that comes my way. I want to get right with You again.*

When she opened her eyes again, she felt renewed. She was going to get through tomorrow, one way or another.

NINETEEN

Trent tugged on his uniform: blue pants and a button-up blue shirt with the name of the HVAC company—Thomas and Sons—proudly displayed on a label. He had to make sure everything was in place before he stepped inside the annals of the art gallery.

The McAllister Gallery was no mom-and-pop storefront. No, it was a grand building located in Arlington, and no expense had been spared. The exterior appeared to be marble and stone, the shrubs were well manicured and the entrance had a pricey-looking statue out front.

Trent slammed the door of his van. It was a plain, nondescript white one that could easily pass as one of the HVAC company's. He had the van for his PI work, and it had come in handy on more than one occasion. Thanks to an old friend, he'd also been able to collect some of the basic heating and air-conditioning supplies, including an anemometer to test airflow. He'd picked them up last night and gotten a rundown on HVAC basics.

Now it was time to put his plan into action. This was where the rubber met the road. This could blow everything open or end very poorly.

He prayed it was the former.

Adjusting the bag on his shoulder, he approached the back door. Even the back of this place looked nice and well kept, with not a speck of dirt in sight.

He hit the back doorbell, a tremor of anxiety rushing through him. Some nerves were healthy, he reminded himself, especially in situations like this. A touch of fear kept a person sharp and alert; it helped the fight or flight kick in.

A trim woman wearing a stylish black business suit pulled the door open. She held a clipboard and pushed up her dark plastic-framed glasses when she spotted Trent. "Can I help you?"

"Ms. Clark, I'm here with Thomas and Sons HVAC. We had an appointment." It paid off that Tessa had done her research and discovered this woman's name. It lent credibility to him being here.

The woman tilted her head, studying him for a moment. "I don't recall an appointment."

"We come out twice a year to check out your system as part of your service plan. We scheduled this in advance, but our secretary, Barbara, should have called to confirm the appointment."

"Right, Barbara." That seemed to appease the woman a moment. She stepped back and allowed Trent inside.

Obstacle number one: check.

He only had about fifty more to get past before he could breathe easy again.

"You must be new. I haven't seen you before."

Trent flashed what he hoped was a charming smile. "I am. I've never been here before, but my girlfriend loves this place. I've been meaning to bring her here sometime."

He glanced around, hoping that he wouldn't see anyone he recognized—or anyone who recognized him, for that matter. Even with his hat on and the uniform covering him, there was little else he could do to conceal how he looked.

"Well, there's not much to see here behind the curtain except a lot of boxes and cleaning supplies." She spread her hand to showcase the back office area around them. "But beyond this area is fantastic. We feature some world-renowned artists, including Alejandro Gaurs."

She tucked a hair behind her ear. "Anyway, the thermostat is over there." She pointed to the wall next to an interior door.

"I'll need to check each of the vents, also." He raised the anemometer. "I run the meter over them so I can make sure they're running at full capacity. This harsh weather we've had already can overtax heating systems. It's better to discover it now than to wait until something goes wrong. Then you'll just have a lot of cold visitors to the gallery. No one wants that."

"Of course. No problem. Is that where you'd like to start?"

"That would be great."

"This way," Ms. Clark said to him.

Trent followed her out of the back office and into a hallway. Four doors were located there. The offices, he realized. This was exactly where he needed to be.

As he passed one of the doors, he heard someone talking on the other side. Two or three voices. All men. At least one seemed to have an accent. Could it be Leo and some of his cohorts?

Any relief he'd felt earlier disappeared. This could get sticky, and fast.

Ms. Clark opened the door. "This is my office. How about you start here?"

"Sounds great."

"I'm just going to step out to the restroom. I'll be right back."

"Sounds great." He walked over to the vent and held his meter over it.

As soon as she disappeared, he put his equipment down and quickly pulled up the vent.

If this didn't work, then Trent didn't know what they would do. This was their only lead and at times it seemed like their only chance.

He pulled out a flashlight and shone it down into the dark recesses of the vent.

He saw nothing.

Wasting no time, he reached his hand down into the metal shaft. He felt around carefully. If there was something down there, he didn't want to send it deeper into the duct.

Nothing.

He reached a little farther, knowing he was on borrowed time.

His fingers connected with something.

Could it be…?

His hand emerged from the vent. A flash drive was wedged between his fingers.

Bingo! The device had still been there, and Leo had been clueless about it the whole time.

Just as he slid it into his pocket, he heard movement behind him.

He turned in time to see Ms. Clark standing there, staring at him with obvious distrust. "What are you doing?" she demanded.

Trent had to think quickly.

Tessa was walking on eggshells. Her mind wouldn't stop racing as she thought about what

Trent was doing at the moment. She paced the house, ran through scenarios in her mind, prayed.

It felt good to pray, especially since her life had been so absent of faith recently. Giving her cares to a higher being brought great comfort. But even with her renewed trust in God, there was still the human aspect of living—the fear that wanted to creep in, the uncertainty and the anxiety.

Lord, please watch over Trent.

Best she could tell, she'd gone onto Leo's server undetected last night. Trent was risking his life for her, and she wanted to do whatever she could to ensure his safety.

A small niggle of doubt still crept into her psyche, though. There were so many uncertainties, so many things she couldn't be sure about.

She allowed herself to dream for a moment about what life would be like without living under this kind of strain. Even more so, how much safer the world would be without a family like the McAllisters out there, smuggling out blueprints for weapons that would destroy lives. This whole thing was bigger than her. Bigger than her family. Bigger than the McAllisters, even.

With the right evidence, maybe the authorities would believe her. Maybe they would take her off the wanted list and actually take action against this powerful crime family.

Then there was a chance she and Trent could

truly explore a relationship together. The idea of beginning something like that in the midst of all of this craziness seemed like a bad idea. Their emotions were just too heightened and enlarged.

Zach walked into the room at that moment.

"Did you hear anything?" Tessa asked, turning her full attention on him.

He shook his head. "Not yet. I wish we'd had more time and resources. We could have wired him or put a camera on him. But we couldn't do that. So we just wait instead."

"Do you really think this is going to work?" Tessa dared to ask. She wanted more than anything to believe that this was possible. But then the fear came. The fear of something happening to Trent, of being discovered, of Leo capturing her and exacting his torturous revenge.

"If anyone can do it, it's Trent. I know the stress right now is probably overwhelming, but all we can do is wait."

"I'd rather be doing something."

"The safest thing you can do right now is to stay right here. All we can do is trust that God is in control right now and that all things will work out the way they're supposed to."

"Even when the lives of millions of people are on the line," she whispered.

He squeezed her shoulder. "Even when the lives of millions are on the line. It's a tough world we live in, filled with hard stuff. Stuff that makes you sick and turns your stomach."

"So we cling to the unseen instead of what we see here in this world," Tessa said.

"Exactly." Zach settled against the wall. "You know, Trent is a great guy. He was devastated after what happened with Laurel. I didn't know if he'd ever fall in love again."

"He's not in love," Tessa was quick to say.

"Maybe not yet. But he's on his way. I can tell by the way he's acting. I'm really happy for him."

Tessa let his words sink in. Could he be telling the truth?

Even more so, this conversation made Tessa realize something else: against all odds, she was beginning to fall in love with Trent, too.

Trent stood and held up a wad of dust and dried leaves from the ficus tree nearby. "There was quite a bit of dust in this duct. I pulled the cover off so I could get a more accurate reading. Tell me, does it get cold in here often?"

The woman shifted. "I suppose I do always wear my sweater. I thought I was just cold natured."

He shook his head. "No, these vents need to be cleaned out. Of course, that's more than I can do today, but I'd guess some of the ductwork under the building may need to be touched up.

The temperature in here should be sixty-eight, but it's only sixty-two."

She shivered at his words. "I'm glad I'm not going crazy. I always felt like a whiner when I brought up how chilly I was."

He tucked his meter back into pocket. "Don't worry. I'll have everything checked out. I'm going to have to come out with some help, though. This is more than a one-person job. It is covered by your warranty, so price shouldn't be an issue."

"Price usually doesn't matter with Mr. McAllister anyway, but that's good to know. It will be one less channel I have to go through, since there's no budget approval needed. When can we schedule you?"

"I'll have to get Barbara to give you a call back. I'll mention it to her when I get into the office."

"Thanks for coming in."

Trent's heart slowed for a minute. If he could just get out of here and into his van, he'd be home free. He'd take this information to his contact with the FBI, and then he'd pray that everything else fell into place.

He took a step into the hallway and balked. Leo McAllister stepped out of the office, two men behind him. Trent tugged his hat down lower, but made sure to keep his chin up. He couldn't afford to look guilty or bring any unnecessary attention to himself.

Leo didn't seem to see him. He continued to talk to the two men beside him as he walked down the hallway toward him. He did cast a look of approval at his secretary before mentioning something else about a shipment they had coming in.

He'd just taken one step past Leo when the man paused.

"You're with the HVAC company?" Leo said.

Trent composed himself and turned halfway. The man had talked to him before, but only once and only briefly. Still, there was a chance he might recognize Trent. "That's right. Just doing some maintenance."

Leo stared at him, something cold, hard and unreadable in his eyes.

Trent steadied his breathing. Had he been made?

TWENTY

Why hadn't Trent called yet?

Tessa continued pacing the living room. He'd been gone for three hours now. Certainly that was enough time to get in and out. So why hadn't he made contact?

Zach was talking to a former colleague on the phone, trying to ascertain the best person to hand over the information to once they had it.

This seemed like the longest day of Tessa's life.

Lord, please watch over him. Keep him safe.

She walked over to the window and peered outside, hoping to see Trent coming down the lane. Instead, she saw a yard covered with pristine snow.

It really was beautiful out here. Under different circumstances, there'd be so much to enjoy about being here. But at the moment it felt desolate and isolated and like a prison.

Much like what her life had felt like for the past year.

Desperate to keep her thoughts occupied, she began to review everything she would tell the authorities once Trent returned with the information. She would leave no detail out. She knew the names of associates, dates of business trips abroad, large sums of money that had been exchanged. Of course, all that meant nothing without proof.

When Trent returned—because he would return, she told herself—he would have that evidence to finally nail Leo.

Her gaze paused at something in the distance. She squinted, uncertain if she was seeing things. But down by the tree line, she thought she'd seen movement.

She shook her head. No, she must have been seeing things. She looked closer, stared harder, but all she saw was trees. Underbrush. Dark recesses.

If there had been movement, it was just the wind. Maybe a bird. It could even be a deer.

She was so used to living in fear.

But there was no way she could have been discovered here. She'd taken every precaution yesterday when she'd accessed those computer files. She'd redirected the server, made dummy locations, the works.

She stared at that spot in the distance again until finally her heart slowed. She was overreacting. She hoped her paranoia would soon become a distant memory.

"We've been having hot and cold spots. I'm glad you're here," Leo said.

As he walked away, Trent tried to relax. But when he heard the man's phone ring, his steps slowed.

"You're there now?" Leo said into the phone. "Perfect. Bring her to the location we discussed. We'll go from there."

Tessa? Was he talking about Tessa? There was no way she could have been discovered.

"Are you okay, sir?" Ms. Clark said.

He nodded and kept walking. Better not to draw any attention to himself. Besides, that wouldn't stop anything that was happening at the house. That would only delay him getting back to Tessa.

"So you'll be in touch?" the woman said.

He gave her an assuring smile. "Definitely."

"Great. Stay warm out there. I hear there's more snow coming."

He walked calmly back to the van, placed his supplies in the back and then climbed inside. To err on the side of caution, he started the van and pulled out of the parking lot. He stopped the next block down and pulled out his phone.

Zach picked up on the first ring. "What's going on?"

"Where's Tessa?"

"In the living room. Worrying. Why?"

"I think Leo's men know where she is."

"That's impossible."

"I don't know what happened, but I need you to be careful. Very careful. I'm on my way there now."

Before he hung up the phone, he heard a gunshot sound on the other end the line.

Tessa heard glass break at the other end of the house and her heartbeat ratcheted.

She didn't even take time to examine possible alternate causes for the noise. She only knew trouble was here.

The sound had come from the end of the house where Zach was staying.

She grabbed the gun from the table where she'd left it, held it near her chest and rushed toward the door. Moving slowly, carefully, she checked down the hallway. It looked clear.

She moved quietly down the corridor, clearing each room as she went. She knew where she needed to go: Zach's room, at the end of the hallway. She dreaded what she would find when she got there. In her heart, she already knew it wouldn't be good.

With trembling hands, she searched the second-to-last room. It was clear.

Finally, she approached the closed door to Zach's room.

Part of her wanted to run. To flee. To stick her head in the sand.

But she couldn't do that. Trent and Zach both had gone out of their way to help her. She couldn't abandon either of them now.

It was silent on the other side of the doorway. That realization in itself sent a shudder through her.

Had a shot been fired through the window, hitting Zach and rendering him immobile? Or were there men inside, crouching and waiting to attack?

Drawing in a deep breath and trying to summon her courage, she held her gun in position and pushed the door open. To her dismay, she spotted Zach. He was on his knees. Hands behind his back. Blood trickled down his forehead and his shirt had red stains. He hadn't been shot—not yet. But the window was shattered behind him.

A man stood on the other side of him, a gun to Zach's forehead. Tessa recognized him as one of the men who'd been chasing them.

How had they been discovered? Was it because of the computer transmission? Had she led the men here? Had she invited death into this place of safety?

"Don't do it, Tessa," Zach said, his voice scratchy and low.

"Nice to see you could join us," the man said.

Three other men appeared in the room, all with guns in their hands. There was no way she could handle all of them. The moment she pulled the trigger, someone else with a gun would shoot her and then Zach. It was a no-win situation.

"How'd you find us?" she asked, her gaze flinging from Zach to the man holding the gun beside him.

"Did you think we wouldn't notice if someone got onto our server? We hired the best IT guys, just in case you tried to do something like that again. As soon as you logged in, we traced your location."

Her heart twisted with grief. This was her fault.

And what about Trent? Was he in danger now, too?

"What we can't figure out is why you logged on. Certainly you're smart enough to know we removed all of that information that was on there," the man continued.

She shrugged, trying to keep a cool head. "I have my reasons."

"Maybe you should start sharing." The man cocked the gun and shoved it into Zach's temple.

"No!" she shouted, fear pulsing through her. "He's done nothing wrong. I'm the one you want."

"Don't listen to them, Tessa," Zach said.

"This is my battle, Zach. Not yours. Not Trent's." She said the words with resignation. But she knew they were true. She couldn't live with herself if someone died because of her.

"Smart thinking," the man with the gun muttered. "Now put your weapon down."

Slowly, Tessa lowered it to the floor and then rose again with her hands in the air. "Let him go."

The man motioned to his thugs. Two of them grabbed Tessa and zip-tied her arms behind her with more than necessary roughness. She squirmed in discomfort.

This was it, she realized. The moment when she couldn't go back. The moment when she had to face her greatest fears.

Her eyes connected with Zach's and she saw the concern there. This wasn't what Trent would have wanted. But she had no other choice. No one else was going to get killed because of her.

The man in charge took the butt of his gun and slammed it into Zach's head. Tessa sucked in a quick breath, alarm rushing through her. As Zach's head slumped, she let out a moan.

She started to lunge toward him, but the man beside her jerked her back.

"Let's go," the man in charge said.

Tessa took one last fleeting glance at Zach before the men dragged her out the door and into a waiting SUV.

TWENTY-ONE

Trent drove faster than he should have. But he had to get to Tessa before Leo's men did. He'd tried calling Zach back, but there had been no answer. His blood pressure heightened to unhealthy levels as he imagined what might be happening.

He swerved into the driveway and saw an eerily calm house ahead. As he jumped from the driver's seat, he drew his gun. He crept around to the back of the house and saw the broken window.

That was when his fears were confirmed. Something bad had happened here.

He hurried to the back door, surveyed the area on the other side of the glass. It appeared to be clear. He quietly opened it and stepped inside.

Silence greeted him.

He had a feeling everyone was gone, but he still had to be careful.

At least in the kitchen, there was no evidence of a struggle. As he stepped into the dining room, he didn't see blood or broken furniture. But the twisted feeling remained in his gut.

He searched each room as he traveled down the hall.

That was when he spotted Zach.

His friend lay on the floor, his arms tied, a chair behind him. Blood streamed from his forehead, his eye was swollen and he seemed to just be returning to consciousness.

Trent rushed toward him and untied his arms.

"They got her. I'm sorry," his friend croaked.

"We need to get you to a hospital."

"I'll be okay. We have to find her. They'll kill her, Trent."

Zach's words ignited something in him. His feelings for Tessa had grown quickly. But that didn't mean they were any less real. He couldn't lose someone else he was beginning to care about.

His thoughts flashed through his mind at an alarming rate. He was charged up and ready to find her. But where?

"I'm going with you." Zach pulled himself up with a wince.

"I can't ask you to do that."

"I'm not giving you a choice."

Trent accepted this with a quick nod. There was no time to argue. "Okay, let's go, then."

Trent's mind raced as he hurried to the van. Not the fastest vehicle, but it would have to work.

They climbed in, and as he cranked the engine, he turned toward Zach. "Tell me what you know."

"There were six of them. They all had guns. And they were unapologetic."

"Any hints on where they went?" He pulled onto the road.

"No idea."

Certainly they hadn't taken Tessa back to the gallery. But where else would they have taken her?

He thought back and remembered that address they'd found in the car they'd taken from the fake cops. Could they have taken her there? He didn't know, but he didn't have any other ideas at the moment.

"Can you pull up Wilmington Heights, Virginia, on your phone?" he asked Zach.

"I know where that is. Probably forty-five minutes from here. Why?"

"It's my best guess as to where they might have gone. We found an address in the car when those men impersonating police officers arrested us. How far do you think it is from the art gallery in DC?"

"Maybe fifteen minutes?"

The idea solidified in his mind. It was worth a shot.

He prayed he was right.

* * *

Tessa couldn't see where they were taking her. They'd thrown something over her head, a black bag of some sort. She was in the trunk, where she couldn't even hear their conversation, except for occasional laughter. These men were enjoying their job a little too much.

At first, she tried to pay attention to every bump, every turn. But after a while, she lost track. There were too many twists and turns, and she felt as if she'd been in the trunk for hours.

She steadied her breathing. How long had it been? An hour? Less? More?

She'd lost her sense of time.

The moment she stopped paying attention to the things she had control over was the moment panic started creeping in. That was when she started imagining seeing Leo again and thinking about what he might do with her.

He'd be angry. He'd had a long time to let his anger simmer, too. It had most likely only increased with time.

Think, Tessa. Think. Remain in control.

Where would they be taking her?

They were too smart to go to Leo's house, or any of his registered properties, for that matter.

Finally, the car rolled to a stop. Another surge of panic started in her. Her heart raced as she prepared to face the unknown.

She felt the trunk open as a *whoosh* of air rushed inside. Then strong hands grabbed her and jerked her from the vehicle. Despite the fact that her legs felt like gelatin, she managed to stand.

Two men pulled her down a sidewalk. She couldn't walk fast enough to keep up. Then she heard a door open and she was shoved inside a building. They led her across a slick floor.

Pay attention, Tessa.

She could smell motor oil. Maybe cinnamon. Someone was talking in the distance.

The space was still cold, even though she was inside now.

Based on the echo of footsteps, she imagined the space to be open, airy and uncluttered.

Was she in a warehouse of some sort?

Finally, someone shoved her into a chair. She flinched as her back hit the wood there.

Then the bag over her head was snatched away.

She blinked at the bright light. Squinted at the men surrounding her. Squinted when she saw… Leo.

Trent pulled into the town of Wilmington Springs. He remembered the address Tessa had read to him. 123 Arnold Drive.

"Bad news," Zach said. "There is no 123 Arnold Drive."

"They had to use an address to register the car with the DMV."

"You know people fake documents like that all the time, right?"

Trent nodded, coming to a stop at a red light and resisting the urge to punch his steering wheel with frustration. "Yeah, I know."

"We've got to think. Maybe the address they chose has some kind of significance."

Trent racked his brain, trying to remember that conversation. "There was a name associated with it. Tom Tracy."

"I'll look him up and see if I can find out anything." Zach punched something into his phone. "What do you know? There is a Tom Tracy living in Wilmington Heights."

"Address?"

"Looks like it's 121 Arthur Avenue. It's so similar that no one would probably think twice about it if he was pulled over."

"Clever. Now tell me how to get there."

They zipped down the road, the tension between Trent's shoulders growing by the moment. He needed a plan for what he would do when he got there. Zach was too injured to help. Which left Trent pretty much on his own.

He had confidence in his abilities, but he had

to be smart. One man against at least six—probably more—was a bad idea.

"Zach, I need you to call my friend with the FBI."

"You know they might arrest her, right?"

"I know. But without backup she'll be dead. I have hope that when they hear her story, they'll understand. I know Leo has planted evidence against Tessa. But there's a lot of proof here to convict Leo, too."

"Okay," Zach said, raising his phone to make the call.

Trent slowed as they pulled up to an aluminum-sided building in the distance. A chain-link fence, at least nine feet high, surrounded it, and there were no other structures around.

This looked like the perfect place for Leo and his men to plan their nefarious operations.

He pulled off the road and into the woods, hopefully where no one would spot them.

"Zach, if anything happens, I need you to turn this over to the authorities." Trent slid the jump drive into his friend's hand. At least if he and Tessa didn't make it out of this, Leo could still pay for his actions and they could save the lives of thousands of people by unveiling these terrorists and their plans.

"Trent, you should wait until backup gets here."

He shook his head. "I can't. Tessa could be in there. Waiting could mean losing her."

Zach stared at him a moment before letting out a breath. "Let's go, then."

"You're staying here. With this jump drive. You're not in a position to help me right now. I think you have some broken ribs and maybe even a concussion. The best thing you can do for me is to be a lookout."

Zach winced as if pain rushed through him again. Finally, he nodded. "Okay. Be careful, man. I'll be praying."

"Okay."

Trent stepped out, ready to save the woman he loved.

"Well, hello, my darling," Leo crooned, a wickedly charming smile on his face.

Tessa didn't even try to hold back her sneer. She jerked against the zip ties that kept her in her chair, knowing it would do no good. His face was not a welcome one.

He ran a finger down her jawline. "You left so abruptly all those months ago. I didn't have a chance to say goodbye."

Leo looked as slick as ever. He had thick blond hair, perfect teeth and tanned skin that looked as fake as his smile. His clothes were expensive, and he had cultured motions.

She pulled away from his touch. "That's because I never wanted to see you again."

"Well, you don't always get what you want, do you?" He dropped his hand back to his side.

"Why'd you bring me here?"

"Isn't that obvious? To make you pay."

"Just kill me," she seethed.

"That would be too easy."

"You just want to revel in your supposed brilliance."

The smile disappeared from his face. He slid his fingers to the base of her neck and tightened them. "You think you're so smart, don't you? What did you do with all of the information you stole from me?"

She tried to suck in a breath, but he squeezed out her ability to speak. She pushed back her panic, though. She wouldn't give him that satisfaction. Not yet.

"I don't have it," she croaked.

"Then, where is it?"

"It's gone."

"Do I need to do something to jolt your memory?" He leaned closer, his glare deepening.

How could she have ever thought he was handsome? He was conniving and selfish. "I couldn't let you kill innocent people. Thousands of them. Millions, maybe. There were things at stake more important than my safety."

He let go of her and coolly walked away, letting out a detached laugh. "I have to admit, you still impress me. Just like you did when we were engaged."

"That was my first mistake."

His laugh increased. "And you're still feisty. I feared you might lose some of your spirit. I always thought we were good together."

"You're delusional."

"We could still be good together, you know. We could forget all of this. Go and live our happy-ever-after together. What do you think?"

The thought turned her stomach. "I think you're crazy."

"Have it your way, then. My way was much more enjoyable." He paced in front of her and his gaze burned into her. "You did a better job hiding than I thought you would. I figured my men would find you the first week you were gone. There are so many means to track people nowadays after all."

"You were very clever, keeping tabs on my mom. I'm surprised she didn't see through you. The one thing I still don't understand is this— why? Why would you side with men who want to kill? Why would you go through all of this trouble?"

"Do you know what kind of money is available when you smuggle blueprints for weapons of mass destruction, drones and chemical agents?"

"But you're already rich."

"One can never have too much money," he said.

"This has to be about more than that." She simply couldn't fathom someone going to these extremes to obtain more cash. Then again, money had never had a big appeal for her like it did for some.

"Enough talking." He abruptly snapped back into homicidal-maniac mode. "I've thought long and hard about this. Bernard is going to help you understand what a waste of time and resources your betrayal has been. Bernard."

A man stepped forward. He didn't look as imposing as she might have thought. In fact, he appeared to be less than five feet tall. He was scrawny, with greasy hair and a receding hairline.

Then he flashed his knife.

Blood rushed through Tessa as she braced herself for whatever was about to come.

TWENTY-TWO

Trent managed to find an unlatched door. He stepped into a warehouse type of building that had been broken up into smaller spaces. The lights were dim and fluorescent, creating a subtle buzz.

He held his gun close as he gently closed the door behind him. He didn't see anyone, but he had to be careful.

Somewhere in the distance he heard murmuring.

What was this place used for? Was this where they ensured the artwork actually contained blueprints for top secret weapons? Was this place where all of the operations were based?

He didn't have time to ponder it now.

Footsteps came closer.

He pressed himself against the wall near the corner, his heart rate increasing with anticipation. Just as a man stepped toward the door, Trent brought the butt of his gun down on his head. With a moan, the man sank to the floor, out cold.

He grabbed the man's gun and slid it into the back of his waistband. One man down; how many more to go? He wished he knew.

Cautiously he moved forward. If Zach had called his contact with the FBI, then there was a possibility they could be here as soon as ten or fifteen minutes. That was good, because time was of the essence here.

He heard voices coming his way—at least two different people. He ducked into a room—a dark room with various boxes lined against the wall. And paintings. There were paintings in here.

He peered through the crack in the door and saw Leo passing.

"What are you going to do with her once we're done?" the other man asked.

"Dispose of her body," Leo said. "I'm thinking the ocean. Make it look like a suicide. With any luck, her body will be sucked out to sea and no one will ever find it."

"What about that man who's been traveling with her?"

"We can take care of him. He'll be tougher because of his connections with law enforcement. If he makes any accusations against us, we'll deny it. It's not as if he has any proof."

The men's voices faded, but the fire inside Trent grew. He had to get to Tessa. Now.

Once the hallway was silent again, he stepped

out. He kept his steps light as he headed toward the opposite end of the building.

The voices he'd heard in the distance became louder. He was getting closer.

Finally, he paused outside a door.

A scream sounded inside.

Tessa.

That was Tessa.

He had to get to her.

When Tessa felt the knife prick the skin on her wrist and then saw the red blood appear, she couldn't stop the scream from surging out from her throat. She could try to be tough all she wanted, but pain was pain.

With a new faith in Christ, she wasn't afraid of death. However, the process of dying seemed terrifying. Besides, when she thought of her family, she had a reason to live. When she thought about Trent, she knew she wanted more than anything to explore what a relationship with him might be like.

Bernard smiled at her again. He was missing teeth and the few he had were brown or yellowed. Her arm ached after the first cut. She knew there was more to come.

Against her will, tears rushed to her eyes.

She fought against the restraints, trying to get

away. She knew her effort was futile, but she didn't stop trying.

"Struggling will only make this more painful," Bernard said, displaying a crooked smile.

"It's too bad Leo isn't enough of a man to do this himself. He has to get you to do his dirty work."

Bernard chuckled. "I'll pass on the message. But until then, we have other business to attend to." He stepped closer.

A groan escaped her lips, belying her defiant tone.

Just as he lowered his knife toward the skin on her other arm, the door burst open.

In a flurry of events, she spotted Trent. His gun was raised. Quickly, he pulled the trigger, first hitting Bernard and then the other two men in the room. Each of them moaned with pain, clutching their shoulders or knees. Not lethal shots, but shots meant to hinder, to slow down their efforts. She could respect that.

A tear of joy cascaded down her cheek. Trent was here. Maybe she did have a reason to hope she might survive.

Moving quickly, he grabbed Bernard's knife and cut the ties around her arms. "Are you okay?" he asked, tenderness softening his voice.

She nodded. "Better now that you're here."

He glanced down at her arm and blanched.

As Bernard started to sit up, Trent slammed his fist against the man's head and he slumped back to the ground. "We've got to get out of here. Now."

She nodded, knowing better than to argue.

Trent pulled her out of the chair, glanced around and then walked toward the door. He scanned the hallway before leading her out. "You know another way to leave this place?"

"I was blindfolded. No idea."

He led her down the hallway. Footsteps and shouts sounded in the distance.

Tessa knew that with the gunfire, Leo would quickly discover what had happened. They didn't have much time.

They reached the end of the hallway. It was a dead end.

This wasn't good.

She looked up at Trent and saw the contemplation on his face. Finally, he pulled her into a room off the hallway and put a finger over his lips to signal silence. She froze, hardly able to breathe as she listened to the footsteps coming closer.

How many men had she seen? There were at least three or four more. Could Trent handle them on his own?

Now that they were on to the fact that Trent was here, it seemed unlikely. They were too outnumbered.

But she wouldn't give in to despair. There was no time for that.

"Where could they have gone?" a voice that clearly belonged to Leo exploded. "Find them. Now. Kill them when you do. I don't have time for any more of these games."

Trent's grip on her biceps tightened and he shoved her farther behind him. He had his gun in his hands.

"Check the rooms!"

Tessa's heart rate quickened.

Slowly, Trent leaned down and grabbed a metal doorstop from the floor. With measured movements, he tossed it down the hallway. The men turned toward the sound. When they did, Trent stepped out and fired.

Tessa gasped at the sound. Her ears would be ringing for days. If she lived that long.

He emerged into the hallway and kicked the men's guns out of the way. Tessa grabbed one and raised it.

They took a step down the hallway. Just then, a man stepped out behind Tessa. His arm went around her neck and, with one squeeze, her gun clattered to the floor.

Trent turned and spotted the beefy man who'd grabbed Tessa. He raised his gun.

"Let her go," he ordered.

"Put the gun down or I'll kill her," the man said.

"I'd do what he says," someone with a smooth voice said behind Trent.

Trent didn't have to look over his shoulder to know it was Leo speaking. His gut told him that the man had a gun pointed at him.

He took one last glance at Tessa, hoping she could read the apology in his eyes. Terror stained her gaze, clutching his heart with grief at the sight.

"Put the gun down," the man behind him said again.

"Don't do it, Trent," Tessa said, her voice raspy and strained.

"I don't have a choice."

"They'll…kill…you," she whispered.

"If I don't put this down, they'll kill you," he said. "I'm sorry I let you down."

Slowly, he raised his free hand and lowered the gun to the floor. He couldn't take the chance. But he didn't know how he was going to get out of this.

Leo strode closer. "Well, wasn't that a beautiful display of young love. You both just made my job easier. I thought I was going to have to track you down, too, but you showed up here. Now I don't have to. I like it when things are easy."

"You're not going to get away with this," Trent assured him.

Leo shrugged. "Sure I will. I always do. With money, you can get away with a lot of things. Everything is going to look like Tessa is behind it. I'll testify that I caught her using my business to do arms deals. I've even had some photos altered to show her meeting in the park with a member of a terrorist group. I always say, leave no stone unturned. It's why I'm so good at what I do. It's all in the details."

The man's cockiness set his nerves on edge.

Tessa gasped for air in the other man's grip. Blood from her wound dripped on the floor, and her face took on a pale hue.

"Let her go!" Trent said, desperate to reach her, to protect her.

Leo chuckled beside him. "I need to make her pay for what she did to me. Don't you understand that? Haven't your investigative skills come in handy at all?" He paced around him. "You're in love with her, aren't you?"

"I'm smart enough to know that love means not hurting or using or mistreating the object of your affection."

"Life is too short not to use people to your advantage." Leo's smile disappeared as he nodded toward the man holding Tessa. "Now finish the job."

Just as Leo said the words, he raised his gun at Trent.

As instinct kicked in, Trent swung his foot and knocked the gun from Leo's hands. Wasting no time, Trent grabbed the weapon and aimed it at Tessa's attacker. The bullet hit him in the throat. The shot was enough to loosen the man's hold on Tessa. She crumpled to the ground, crawling away from the man.

Just as the man reached for her, Trent took another shot, hitting his shoulder. The thug howled with pain.

When Trent turned back around, he saw that Leo had grabbed his gun again and was pointing it right at him.

He dived out of the way, knowing he probably wouldn't make it in time.

Tessa let out a cry and lunged toward Leo. She hit his knees just as he fired. The bullet veered past Trent, skimming the sleeve of his jacket.

"Freeze. FBI!" Four men appeared down the hallway.

Help was here. Help was finally here.

As soon as Leo and his men had been cleared from the building and taken into police custody, Tessa turned to Trent. She had so much she needed to say, but words didn't seem adequate at the moment. He'd saved her life, given her hope for the future and restored her faith in people. How could she show her gratitude for all of that?

She settled for "Thank you."

His hand covered her neck and jaw as he looked tenderly into her eyes. His look showed warmth and love and a depth of emotion that couldn't be faked. "You gave me a good scare."

"I know, but—"

Before she could finish her sentence, his lips covered hers. Time seemed to stand still around them. Everyone else disappeared. Memories of the atrocity that had occurred vanished. At the moment, it was just Trent and Tessa.

"I'd do anything for the woman I love," Trent whispered when they pulled away. "Anything. I hope you've realized that over the past several days."

Her heart raced at his proclamation. She wrapped her arms around his waist. "I love you, Trent. I never thought I would be able to say that. But, against all the odds, here I am. I've never meant the words more."

"You two ready to give a statement?" the agent in charge asked behind them.

Trent kept his arm around Tessa as they turned toward the man.

"I'm ready to share everything I know," Tessa said. "Especially now that Leo is behind bars."

"We've had surveillance on Leo and his men for quite some time. I'm hoping that we have the evidence now to put him away for good."

"After we get done here, what do you say we go see your family?" Trent asked.

Warmth spread from her heart to the rest of her body. "I think that would be the most wonderful thing ever...especially with you by my side."

He smiled before kissing her forehead. "Then, let's get this over with."

EPILOGUE

Six months later

Tessa flipped off the TV after watching the evening news, and a satisfied smile washed across her face. She looked up at Trent, who sat beside her on the couch, and saw that he shared the same expression.

With a new sense of relief filling her, she threw her arms around him. "I can't believe it," she whispered. "This really is over."

His arms circled her waist. She still marveled at his strength—both physically and emotionally. He'd been her rock from the day they'd met, and she thanked God every day that their paths had crossed.

The news anchor had just announced what Tessa and Trent had already suspected would happen—Leo McAllister had accepted a plea deal. He'd be going away for a long time, as would the family's contact with the defense contractor. Not only that, but several weapon blueprints had been intercepted before they'd gotten into the wrong hands.

"You can finally get on with your life," Trent said, pulling back and looking her in the eye. There was an undeniable gleam of affection there. "We can finally get on with *our* lives."

Tessa smiled. She liked the sound of that. Ever since Leo had been arrested, Trent had been at her side. He'd seen to it that he was her personal bodyguard until he was absolutely sure Leo was no longer a threat. And Tessa hadn't minded it one bit. She knew beyond a shadow of a doubt that Trent would do whatever he needed to in order to keep her safe. He'd proved that.

She'd never felt so loved or valued by a man before. Nor had she ever felt such an easy trust.

Not only that, but her mom and brother and sister and nieces and nephews were all back in her life. She'd been so happy to see them and catch up and hug them again.

She'd called Salem, also. He was just fine. Tessa had worried about him, worried that Leo might have tracked him down. Thankfully, that hadn't happened.

Life was falling into place again.

She leaned back into the couch. They were at Trent's house right now. Tessa was living with her mom until she started her new job. She was pleased that she'd soon be working for Trent. She'd be helping him with any cyber issues that popped up in the course of his PI work, as well as with coordinating some of his jobs. It wasn't necessarily something she'd seen herself doing, but she enjoyed organizing and coordinating. Even more, she loved working with Trent.

"Tessa?" Trent asked, his voice husky and serious.

She'd told him that she preferred to go by Tessa now. Theresa seemed too much like the person she used to be.

She glanced up at him, noting that there was a new expression in his eyes. She couldn't pinpoint what it was. Excitement? Nervousness? Mischief? "Yes?"

He rubbed his lips together before speaking. "I know the past six months have been a whirlwind. Totally unexpected and surprising and dangerous at times. But I need to ask you something."

She gripped his arms, hoping she never had to be without his embrace. She felt as though she could move mountains with him by her side. She sucked in a breath as she anticipated what he had to say. "Anything."

In one fluid movement, he was down on one knee. "Will you marry me?"

Her eyes widened with delight and surprise. That was when the ring in his hands came into focus. "Really?" She couldn't believe it—she hadn't been hearing things.

His eyes danced. "Really. You've turned my life upside down, Tessa. You made me realize I can love again, that there's life beyond tragedy. I know the circumstances that pulled us together were unconventional, but I'm so glad they led us to where we are today. I want to start a life with you."

"Me, too."

He smiled. "So what do you think? Will you do me the honor of becoming Mrs. Trent McCabe?"

She grinned so widely that it hurt. "Yes! I would be thrilled. Elated."

He laughed as he stood up, slid the ring on her finger and pulled her into a long hug. He twirled her around before putting her back firmly on her feet. Their gazes met, their faces only inches from each other. "I love you, Tessa Davidson."

"I love you, Trent McCabe."

And Tessa knew without a doubt that life had somehow worked out to bring her right to this very minute.

* * * * *

Dear Reader,

Thank you so much for joining me on Tessa and Trent's adventure. I hope you enjoyed getting to know these characters and the beautiful West Virginia mountain setting. I loved Tessa's and Trent's determination to overcome their trials, even when things seemed hopeless.

Isn't it great to think about the idea that God pursues us with the same tenacity as Tessa and Trent were pursued in this book? Thank goodness it's not with deadly intentions, but because God never gives up on us. His love surpasses all that we can imagine, and He even went as far as to die for us to show us His endless love.

I hope you'll enjoy the next book in this series, which will feature Trent's friend Zach Davis. Zach also had appearances in *Desperate Measures* and *Hidden Agenda*, and, boy, is he in for an adventure as he takes a new job as sheriff in the town of Waterman's Reach.

Many blessings to you!

LARGER-PRINT BOOKS!

GET 2 FREE LARGER-PRINT NOVELS PLUS 2 FREE MYSTERY GIFTS

Love Inspired®

Larger-print novels are now available...

YES! Please send me 2 FREE LARGER-PRINT Love Inspired® novels and my 2 FREE mystery gifts (gifts are worth about $10). After receiving them, if I don't wish to receive any more books, I can return the shipping statement marked "cancel." If I don't cancel, I will receive 6 brand-new novels every month and be billed just $5.49 per book in the U.S. or $5.99 per book in Canada. That's a savings of at least 19% off the cover price. It's quite a bargain! Shipping and handling is just 50¢ per book in the U.S. and 75¢ per book in Canada.* I understand that accepting the 2 free books and gifts places me under no obligation to buy anything. I can always return a shipment and cancel at any time. Even if I never buy another book, the two free books and gifts are mine to keep forever.

122/322 IDN GH6D

Name _____ (PLEASE PRINT) _____

Address _____ Apt. #

City _____ State/Prov. _____ Zip/Postal Code

Signature (if under 18, a parent or guardian must sign)

Mail to the **Reader Service:**
IN U.S.A.: P.O. Box 1867, Buffalo, NY 14240-1867
IN CANADA: P.O. Box 609, Fort Erie, Ontario L2A 5X3

**Are you a current subscriber to Love Inspired® books
and want to receive the larger-print edition?
Call 1-800-873-8635 or visit www.ReaderService.com.**

* Terms and prices subject to change without notice. Prices do not include applicable taxes. Sales tax applicable in N.Y. Canadian residents will be charged applicable taxes. Offer not valid in Quebec. This offer is limited to one order per household. Not valid to current subscribers to Love Inspired Larger-Print books. All orders subject to credit approval. Credit or debit balances in a customer's account(s) may be offset by any other outstanding balance owed by or to the customer. Please allow 4 to 6 weeks for delivery. Offer available while quantities last.

Your Privacy—The Reader Service is committed to protecting your privacy. Our Privacy Policy is available online at www.ReaderService.com or upon request from the Reader Service.

We make a portion of our mailing list available to reputable third parties that offer products we believe may interest you. If you prefer that we not exchange your name with third parties, or if you wish to clarify or modify your communication preferences, please visit us at www.ReaderService.com/consumerschoice or write to us at Reader Service Preference Service, P.O. Box 9062, Buffalo, NY 14240-9062. Include your complete name and address.

LILP15

REQUEST YOUR FREE BOOKS!
2 FREE WHOLESOME ROMANCE NOVELS
IN LARGER PRINT
PLUS 2
FREE
MYSTERY GIFTS

✵✵✵✵✵✵✵✵✵✵✵✵✵✵✵✵✵✵✵✵✵

HEARTWARMING™
🌾🌾🌾🌾🌾🌾🌾🌾🌾🌾🌾🌾🌾🌾🌾🌾🌾🌾🌾

Wholesome, tender romances

YES! Please send me 2 FREE Harlequin® Heartwarming Larger-Print novels and my 2 FREE mystery gifts (gifts worth about $10). After receiving them, if I don't wish to receive any more books, I can return the shipping statement marked "cancel." If I don't cancel, I will receive 4 brand-new larger-print novels every month and be billed just $5.24 per book in the U.S. or $5.99 per book in Canada. That's a savings of at least 19% off the cover price. It's quite a bargain! Shipping and handling is just 50¢ per book in the U.S. and 75¢ per book in Canada.* I understand that accepting the 2 free books and gifts places me under no obligation to buy anything. I can always return a shipment and cancel at any time. Even if I never buy another book, the two free books and gifts are mine to keep forever.

161/361 IDN GHX2

Name _____ (PLEASE PRINT)

Address _____ Apt. #

City _____ State/Prov. _____ Zip/Postal Code

Signature (if under 18, a parent or guardian must sign)

Mail to the **Reader Service:**
IN U.S.A.: P.O. Box 1867, Buffalo, NY 14240-1867
IN CANADA: P.O. Box 609, Fort Erie, Ontario L2A 5X3

* Terms and prices subject to change without notice. Prices do not include applicable taxes. Sales tax applicable in N.Y. Canadian residents will be charged applicable taxes. Offer not valid in Quebec. This offer is limited to one order per household. Not valid for current subscribers to Harlequin Heartwarming larger-print books. All orders subject to credit approval. Credit or debit balances in a customer's account(s) may be offset by any other outstanding balance owed by or to the customer. Please allow 4 to 6 weeks for delivery. Offer available while quantities last.

Your Privacy—The Reader Service is committed to protecting your privacy. Our Privacy Policy is available online at www.ReaderService.com or upon request from the Reader Service.

We make a portion of our mailing list available to reputable third parties that offer products we believe may interest you. If you prefer that we not exchange your name with third parties, or if you wish to clarify or modify your communication preferences, please visit us at www.ReaderService.com/consumerchoice or write to us at Reader Service Preference Service, P.O. Box 9062, Buffalo, NY 14240-9062. Include your complete name and address.

HW15

YES! Please send me **The Montana Mavericks Collection** in Larger Print. This collection begins with 3 FREE books and 2 FREE gifts (gifts valued at approx. $20.00 retail) in the first shipment, along with the other first 4 books from the collection! If I do not cancel, I will receive 8 monthly shipments until I have the entire 51-book Montana Mavericks collection. I will receive 2 or 3 FREE books in each shipment and I will pay just $4.99 US/ $5.89 CDN for each of the other four books in each shipment, plus $2.99 for shipping and handling per shipment.*If I decide to keep the entire collection, I'll have paid for only 32 books, because 19 books are FREE! I understand that accepting the 3 free books and gifts places me under no obligation to buy anything. I can always return a shipment and cancel at any time. My free books and gifts are mine to keep no matter what I decide.

263 HCN 2404   463 HCN 2404

Name	(PLEASE PRINT)	

Address		Apt. #

City	State/Prov.	Zip/Postal Code

Signature (if under 18, a parent or guardian must sign)

Mail to the **Reader Service:**
IN U.S.A.: P.O. Box 1867, Buffalo, NY 14240-1867
IN CANADA: P.O. Box 609, Fort Erie, Ontario L2A 5X3

* Terms and prices subject to change without notice. Prices do not include applicable taxes. Sales tax applicable in N.Y. Canadian residents will be charged applicable taxes. This offer is limited to one order per household. All orders subject to approval. Credit or debit balances in a customer's account(s) may be offset by any other outstanding balance owed by or to the customer. Please allow 4 to 6 weeks for delivery. Offer available while quantities last. Offer not available to Quebec residents.

Your Privacy—The Reader Service is committed to protecting your privacy. Our Privacy Policy is available online at www.ReaderService.com or upon request from the Reader Service.

We make a portion of our mailing list available to reputable third parties that offer products we believe may interest you. If you prefer that we not exchange your name with third parties, or if you wish to clarify or modify your communication preferences, please visit us at www.ReaderService.com/consumerschoice or write to us at Reader Service Preference Service, P.O. Box 9062, Buffalo, NY 14269. Include your complete name and address.

behind him, and hurried down a hallway to the laboratory where he had worked with the material. He got a bottle of Clorox bleach and scrubbed the room from top to bottom, washing countertops and sinks, everything, with bleach. He really scoured the place. After he had finished, he found Patricia Webb and told her what he had seen in his microscope. She telephoned her husband and said to him, "Karl, you'd better come quick to the lab. Fred has looked at a specimen, and he's got *worms.*"

Staring at the worms, they tried to classify the shapes. They saw snakes, pigtails, branchy, forked things that looked like the letter *Y,* and they noticed squiggles like a small *g,* and bends like the letter *U,* and loopy *6*s. They also noticed a classic shape, which they began calling the shepherd's crook. Other Ebola experts have taken to calling this loop the eyebolt, after a bolt of the same name that can be found in a hardware store. It could also be described as a Cheerio with a long tail.

The next day, Patricia Webb ran some tests on the virus and found that it did not react to any of the tests for Marburg or any other known virus. Therefore, it was an unknown agent, a new virus. She and her colleagues had isolated the strain and shown that it was something new. They had earned the right to name the organism. Karl Johnson named it Ebola.

Karl Johnson has since left the C.D.C., and he now spends a great deal of his time fly-fishing for